Enter If You Dare

Mr. Schaffer opened the door. The noise inside hit us with a force that nearly bowled us over. How could eight kids make so much noise?

I trailed in behind him, wishing I could disappear. An object hurled at my head. It was only a paper wad, but I was already skittish. I bolted behind the door like a scared rabbit.

Mr. Schaffer dropped his briefcase, sidestepping the paper airplanes that clipped past his ears. "Quiet!" he shouted.

No one paid him any attention. A fat red-haired boy smacked a blond girl with a map puller. The girl kicked over a stack of textbooks and then punched the boy back.

"Okay," Mr. Schaffer shouted. "You've had your fun. In your seats, everybody." No dice. He came over to lead me out from behind the door. "Austin, will you please take a seat?"

I hesitated. "It's all right," he said. "Don't be nervous. You're a student in this class now."

Somehow, that wasn't the least bit reassuring.

THE SPITBALL CLASS

CANDICE F. RANSOM

A MINSTREL® BOOK

PUBLISHED BY POCKET BOOKS

New York   London   Toronto   Sydney   Tokyo   Singapore

This book is a work of fiction. Names, characters, places and incidents either are products of the author's imagination or are used fictitiously. Any resemblance to actual events or locales or persons, living or dead, is entirely coincidental.

A MINSTREL PAPERBACK *ORIGINAL*

A Minstrel Book published by
POCKET BOOKS, a division of Simon & Schuster Inc.
1230 Avenue of the Americas, New York, NY 10020

ISBN: 0-671-72910-1

First Minstrel Books printing March 1994

10 9 8 7 6 5 4 3 2 1

A MINSTREL BOOK and colophon are registered trademarks of Simon & Schuster Inc.

Cover art by Dan Burr

Printed in the U.S.A.

Chapter

1

✻ Nobody in her right mind ever went willingly into Room 24.

Everyone in Freeman Elementary knew about Room 24. The kids in that class were legendary. They had been together since second grade, after driving their first grade teachers bonkers. From second grade on, those kids were permanently assigned to Room 24.

Now the kids in that room were in sixth grade, like me.

I'd heard some really wild stories about the kids in Room 24.

Like, how only the meanest, rottenest, most impossible kids were put in that class. The hard cases.

The kids in Room 24 were so terrible, no teacher ever stayed to teach them. The record stood at three months, two weeks, and four days, held by a teacher who was at Freeman during the flu season. Most of the kids in Room 24, like the kids in the other classes, were out sick, which was why this particular teacher was able to hang on so long.

Or so the story went.

Another time a teacher left in such a hurry she forgot her purse. She claimed the spitballs were flying so thick, it looked like a blizzard, and she refused to teach a Spitball Class. She never came back—the principal mailed her her purse—but the name she made up stuck. Soon everybody called Room 24 the Spitball Class. Rumors about it flew as thick as spitball blizzards.

My mother always told me not to believe rumors. They were just stories, she said, invented by one person who had something to gain by hurting another person, or harmless little incidents that got blown all out of proportion.

My father, on the other hand, told me there was usually a tiny kernel of truth in a rumor, buried deep among layers of lies and half-truths. At that time he was talking about the rumor that a lot of people were going to be laid off at his job. That rumor turned out to have a *big* kernel of truth in it.

That was the reason I was about to discover what *really* went on in Room 24.

Let me back up, though, and start from the beginning.

My name is Austin Sommers. I'm a sixth grader at

Freeman Elementary School, and I'm perfectly normal! There is *nothing* wrong with me.

I'm a *girl,* even though my name sounds like a boy's name, or the name of a city. I was named after the place I was born, Austin, Texas. I have short brown hair and brown eyes, also normal (maybe even boring).

I make pretty good grades (okay, I'm lousy in math), have lots of friends, and I would have been voted vice-president of my class except I wasn't at Freeman the first six weeks of the school year. Elections were held a month after school started.

If I *had* been there, I would have run for office and won, probably. I knew my best friend Erin Shorter would run for class president—she's been class president since third grade. I would have been vice-president, and Patty Wheeler, my other best friend, was a shoo-in for secretary-treasurer. The three of us would have ruled sixth grade.

Not being vice-president wasn't so bad. Missing the first six weeks of school at Freeman wasn't the end of the world, either. I could live with that. What I couldn't live with was being stuck in the Spitball Class.

If I hadn't been in Florida the first part of the year, I'd have been in a regular class. Blame it on palm trees.

During the summer my father had gotten a new job in Orlando, Florida, only a few miles from Disney World. We sold our house in Virginia and moved right before school started. Moving to Florida in August was no trip to the beach (no pun intended). It was so hot the candles Mom packed melted and some of our Christmas tree lights exploded from the heat.

Our new house in Orlando was made of cinder blocks painted pink and had a flat tiled roof. It was like living in a pastel shoe box. There was a wall around our yard that made it seem like a jail compound. Whenever I went out, I felt like I was making a break for it and half expected somebody to yell, "Guards!"

I suppose I would have eventually got used to the house—but never the wildlife. Florida teemed with crawling things. My brother, Chester, loved all of them, but what could you expect from an eight-year-old whose sole purpose in life was to catch creepie-crawlies? There were a lot to catch. Tiny lizards skittered up and down the porch screens, and every kind of bug you can imagine—and some you can't—scampered across my bare feet at one time or another.

Mostly I missed my friends, Erin and Patty. We'd been best friends since third grade, and nobody in my new school came close to them. The kids in Neil Armstrong Middle School wore shorts and sunglasses on cords. Armstrong seemed more like a summer camp than a school.

In other words, I hated Florida.

One day after school I was moping around our gloomy cinder block house when Dad came home early.

A few days before, he had mentioned the rumor about layoffs at his work. The rumor was true, he reported glumly. Fortunately his old company wanted him back, which meant we'd have to move back to Virginia.

I threw my arms around him. "Dad! That's great!"

He blinked in surprise. "You mean you're not upset? Any other kid would be devastated to leave Florida. America's playground."

We'd been to the beach and Disney World five or six times since we moved there. The beach was okay, but I wasn't thrilled by Mickey Mouse, a fact my parents kept forgetting.

Chester was heartbroken when he heard. He threatened to run away and get a job at Reptile Ranch, a park where people actually paid to watch alligators being fed.

"Yes, you'd make some alligator a tasty dinner," I told him. Chester kicked me in the shin, but I didn't care. We were going home!

Mom met Dad's news with a sigh. "Two moves in less than two months. I just finished unpacking. Where are we going to live?" she asked Dad.

Since our house in Virginia had been sold, we couldn't very well ask the people who bought it to get out. Dad solved the problem in his usual no-fuss manner. He proposed renting a townhouse in our old neighborhood so Chester and I could go to our old school, Freeman Elementary.

"All right," Mom agreed. "I'll find us a new house, but I'm going to take my time."

I didn't care if we moved into the nearest police station. We were going *home!*

It didn't take us long to pack, and a moving company took our furniture ahead to Virginia. Through a real estate agent, Dad rented a three-bedroom townhouse near where we used to live.

The trip back north was uneventful, unless you counted the time Chester cut his foot in a motel pool in South Carolina and we had to find an emergency room in a strange town.

The instant we hit Virginia soil, I called Erin. I had already written her and Patty, but I couldn't wait to hear her voice.

"Austin!" she shrieked in my ear. "You're back! This is so incredible! Patty says she still can't believe it."

"I can't believe it myself," I told her. "We're moving to Lake Ridge. One-two-five-oh-six Buggy Whip. Can you come over Sunday evening? I'm dying to find out what's been happening."

"I can't come over Sunday," Erin said regretfully. "We're having a big dinner—one of those family things. You'll be busy anyway, unpacking and all. Patty and I'll see you Monday morning at school, okay?"

"Okay. I'll have to go to the office first and get my class assignment. Maybe I'll be in your room."

"I'll meet you by the main office," Erin promised.

I hung up feeling wonderful. It was so great to be

6

back where I belonged. I couldn't wait until Monday.

True to her word, Erin met me outside the office. She ran over and hugged me.

"Patty wanted to be here, but she had to help Mr. Trocadero in the music room," she said. "She'll see you at lunch."

Patty was in band and hadn't run for class secretary-treasurer after all, Erin said, filling me in. The band kept her pretty busy. But Erin *was* class president. Shawn Zuskin was secretary-treasurer.

"Who's vice-president?" I asked, wondering who had the office that might have been mine, if I'd been here to run.

"A new girl," Erin replied. "Her name is Bailey Hoffman. You'll like her. You won't believe where she lives—"

Just then a first grader charged right into her. I laughed, feeling as excited as the little kid. We went in the office to get my room assignment.

My mother had picked up Chester's and my school records from our Florida school. Mom had taken Chester in to be registered, but I didn't want her to help me reenroll. I'd attended Freeman since kindergarten, so I could do it myself. I rode the bus with the other kids that morning.

Miss Hopkins, the school secretary, came over to greet me as I placed the brown envelope containing my school records on the high counter.

"Hi, Miss Hopkins," I said with a smile. "I'm back!"

"Hello, Austin. Your mother was in early with your brother. I don't think I've ever heard of anybody coming *back* from Florida. People usually go down there and stay. You'll probably be sorry when winter comes."

"I don't think so," I said cheerfully. "I like snow. Which room am I going to be in?"

It was a good thing Erin was with me. When Miss Hopkins told me to report to Room 24, I nearly passed out. Erin helped me back up to the counter.

"You can't mean Room Twenty-*four,*" I said feebly.

"Room Twenty-four," Miss Hopkins repeated.

"Look at your paper again, please," I begged. "There must be a mistake. A typo or something."

She showed me the printout with my class assignment on it. "Room Twenty-four. Right there in black and white. Well, gray and white. The printer needs a new ribbon."

"But—not that room!" I sputtered, panic-stricken. "Room Twenty-four is— I can't possibly be in that class!"

Miss Hopkins left to answer the phone.

I felt the world go black. "Erin!" I wailed. "They put me in the Spitball Class!"

"I can't believe it!" Erin gasped. "How could they do this to you?"

"I don't know!" I was practically crying.

8

"You poor kid," Erin said. "Patty and I were going to save you a place at lunch. Now we'll probably never see you again."

She was a big help.

Miss Hopkins came back and saw I was freaked out over my room assignment. "I'm sorry, Austin. We're pretty tight this year for space. It's the only class with an empty desk. The other sixth-grade classes are hopelessly overcrowded."

"What's one more kid?" I asked desperately. "You can squeeze a desk in Erin's room, can't you?"

"I'm in the T and G room this year," Erin said.

"You are?" I stared at her. She hadn't told me. T and G stood for Talented and Gifted. Erin was smart—after all, she was class president. I shouldn't have been surprised she was in the smart kids' class, but I was still reeling from shock.

"What about Patty's room?"

"She's in T and G, too," Erin replied.

There was no chance I would ever be accepted in the Talented and Gifted program, not with my crummy math grades. But one of the other sixth-grade teachers must have room for one more person. I wasn't very big. I didn't take up much space.

I wrung my hands in despair. "I don't need a desk. I'll sit on the floor. Or on the heating unit. I'll stand, even!"

Miss Hopkins shook her head. "Fire regulations prevent students from sitting on heating units, and

9

building codes say we can't have more than thirty students per room. Room Twenty-four is the only class not filled to the rafters this year. If we had two extra classes, we'd have a double trailer out back. As it is we're overcrowded to be uncomfortable, but not enough to qualify for a trailer."

Did I care about codes and regulations? This was my life!

Miss Hopkins patted my shoulder. "Don't worry. Someone is bound to leave Freeman, and we can transfer you. It's only temporary."

Somehow I didn't feel better.

"You're not the only new person starting today," Miss Hopkins said brightly. She pointed to a tall, dark-haired man coming out of the principal's office. "Your teacher."

The last bell rang. "I've got to run," Erin said. "I'll be late. Bye, Austin. It's been nice knowing you."

"Erin! Wait—" I wanted her to walk me to my class, but she dashed out the door.

"Mr. Schaffer," Miss Hopkins said to the dark-haired man. "Come meet one of your students. This is Austin Sommers."

Mr. Schaffer set his briefcase down to shake my hand. He was young, I noticed, and good-looking. He had trusting brown eyes that reminded me of those of a cocker spaniel.

"Hello, Austin. Glad to meet you." His voice was nice.

"It's Austin's first day, too," Miss Hopkins said. "Austin, why don't you sit over there? When Mr. Schaffer is finished here, you can both go to your new class together."

I sank weakly into a chair just around the corner. What was I going to do? Appeal to a higher court?

"Did Mr. Wren tell you about your assignment?" I heard Miss Hopkins ask Mr. Schaffer. Their voices carried easily around the corner.

"Yes, I understand I have the worst class in the entire school. What do they call it? The Spitball Class?" He laughed as if he thought it was a big joke.

I nearly fell off my chair. Hadn't he heard the story about how one of the teachers last year was practically burned at the stake? It really wasn't a laughing matter.

"You're young and strong," Miss Hopkins observed. "The kids in Room Twenty-four are a little—rambunctious."

"I guess I can handle them." Mr. Schaffer's tone indicated he was still kidding.

I couldn't believe this guy didn't know anything about the Spitball Class. The class was famous.

"There are eight students," Miss Hopkins informed him. "Nine now, counting Austin. Four girls and five boys."

"That doesn't sound too bad. Nine kids. Pretty small class, if you ask me."

"It'll seem like a hundred," Miss Hopkins said.

"I guess I'd better get moving," I heard Mr. Schaffer say. "The bell rang five minutes ago."

"Room Twenty-four is down the hall, past the furnace room."

"My class is next to the boiler room?" Mr. Schaffer asked. "Why is it all the way down there?"

"Well, the clanging pipes drown out the noise from Room Twenty-four."

Mr. Schaffer became serious now. "A joke is a joke, Miss Hopkins, but this is my class we're discussing."

Miss Hopkins's tone was confidential, as if she were revealing a state secret. "It's no joke. Did Mr. Wren tell you that you're not the first teacher this class has had?"

"I gather the teachers frequently request transfers."

"Or quit. You're the third teacher to take this class *this year*. I'm trying to warn you this is no ordinary class."

"I understand there are nine children who are supposedly discipline problems lumped into one room," Mr. Schaffer replied crisply. "Why aren't those students in a regular classroom?"

"Mr. Wren doesn't believe the mainstream approach works when the children get older. Twenty-eight students shouldn't suffer because one or two refuse to behave. So for the last few years he has put all the troublemakers from each grade into separate classes."

"My class."

"Your class," the secretary agreed with him. "They're a handful, all right. Austin Sommers is the only one without a record. It's a shame there isn't room for her in another class. Mr. Wren feels she'll be okay until space opens in one of the regular sixth-grade rooms."

It was more than a shame, I thought. It was *criminal* to send an innocent, unarmed person into the Spitball Class. I wished I had stayed in Florida and taken my chances with the alligators.

Mr. Schaffer appeared around the corner. Was he a little white around the gills, or was that my imagination?

"Miss Sommers," he said. "Shall we go to our new class?"

He held the door open for me. I guess he thought I needed an escort. He wouldn't be much protection. After all, he was only a teacher.

Everybody knew the inmates in the Spitball Class ate teachers for breakfast, but I had no idea what Room 24 did to new *kids*.

I was about to find out.

Chapter
2

❁ The door to Room 24 was closed, but then, it was usually shut, I remembered. Either to keep the inmates in or to protect innocent students from glimpsing the horrors that took place on the other side of the door. I wasn't sure which.

I half expected to see a big padlock attached to the doorknob, the kind used to lock the cages of dangerous animals. But the door to Room 24 looked like any other door in the school, except for the scuff marks around the bottom. It was as if a million feet had tried to kick the door open.

The noise inside was incredible, like the roar from RFK Stadium during a Redskins game when the Redskins scored a touchdown—only louder.

Mr. Schaffer paused with his hand on the knob. I figured he was either steeling himself to enter or mentally reviewing his last will and testament.

I chewed my lower lip, foolishly hoping to see Miss Hopkins sprinting down the hall, shouting that someone had dropped out and there was an opening for me in a regular class.

Someone *did* come running down the hall, but it wasn't the secretary. I recognized Mr. Haver, the custodian. He was heading for the furnace room next door, not because of any emergency, but because he was on break.

"Good morning," Mr. Schaffer greeted him.

Mr. Haver paused long enough to say, "Morning. Oh, you're the new teacher!" before skidding into the boiler room.

There was nothing else to do but go inside.

Mr. Schaffer opened the door. The noise inside hit us with a force that nearly bowled us over. I'd never heard so much yelling, not even on the last day of school. How could eight kids make so much noise?

"Well, let's see what we've got ourselves into," Mr. Schaffer said bravely and walked on in.

My last thought as I trailed behind him was that I should have paid attention when we were studying fractions in third grade. If my math grades weren't so lousy, I'd be in the T and G class with Erin and Patty, doing sane, talented, and gifted things, not worrying about whether I could duck the object hurled at my head.

It was only a paper wad, but I was already skittish.

15

I bolted behind the door like a scared rabbit. No one saw me—they were carrying on too much to notice.

A paper snowstorm was in progress. The Spitball Class was living up to its name.

Mr. Schaffer dropped his briefcase, sidestepping the paper airplanes that clipped past his ears. "Quiet!" he shouted.

No one paid him any attention. Peering around the door, I counted five boys and three girls—just as Miss Hopkins had said—throwing paper and blackboard erasers. There seemed to be a rehearsed quality to their actions. A fat red-haired boy smacked a blond girl with the map puller. As if on cue, the girl kicked over a stack of textbooks before punching the boy back. It was as if they had done this act a dozen times before. It dawned on me they *had*. The kids of Room 24 were putting on a show for the new teacher, probably to scare him off.

This truth must have dawned on Mr. Schaffer, too, because he stood steadfastly by his desk, which had a crudely lettered sign on it that read, "Go home if you know what's good for you." He just stood there and watched the performance. He was obviously waiting for them to run out of steam and settle down on their own, but he didn't realize the stamina of the Spitball Class. They were not going to quit. If anything, they would get louder.

"Okay!" Mr. Schaffer shouted over the ruckus. "You've had your fun. In your seats, everybody." No dice. He came over to lead me out from behind the door. "Austin, will you please take a seat? Maybe the others will follow your example."

I doubted it. More likely, the others would take the *new* target apart, limb by limb.

I stepped out from behind the shelter of the door and approached the desks, which were in a heap in the middle of the floor, as if the kids planned to set fire to them.

Mr. Schaffer turned one right-side up for me. I was still afraid to sit down.

"It's all right," he said reassuringly. "Don't be nervous. You're a student in this class now."

I wasn't the least bit reassured, but I sat down.

The ruckus suddenly halted in midaction. The yelling stopped abruptly as if someone shut off a faucet.

Eight pairs of eyes regarded me warily. I knew the identities of all but one pair. Those eyes were pale and very blue.

I also knew if I wanted to live until lunchtime, I had to say something to break the ice.

"Hi, guys," I said with a shaky wave.

"What're you doing here, Sommers?" asked Jason Cruikshank. Jason had pushed me down on the playground more than once.

Mr. Schaffer began, "This is Austin Sommers—"

"I know *that*," said Jason.

"Never mind her," said Blue Eyes. He had fair hair and a suspicious expression. "Who are you?"

17

"I'm Mr. Schaffer, your new teacher. Now, if you'll all sit down, I'll take roll."

"How come she's in *here?*" The blond boy stared at me. "What'd she do?"

"She just moved here from Florida," Mr. Schaffer replied. I was beginning to feel like a street lamp, the way they were discussing me in the third person. "Austin has some very interesting stories to tell about her life in Florida that I'm sure you'll enjoy hearing, but first let's take roll—"

Now the boy came over to me. "What'd you do to get kicked out of school?" he asked me. "It must have been pretty bad for them to send you all the way up here."

The others laughed.

"I didn't do anything," I replied, rankled by his measuring look. "I was put in this class because it was the only place left, but I don't really belong here. It's a mistake. The instant they find room in another class, I'm leaving." It wouldn't be a minute too soon, I added to myself.

The boy's blue eyes narrowed as he laughed. "That's what you think!"

I had no idea what he meant by that remark. Mr. Schaffer took advantage of the slight pause.

"Okay, let's turn these desks over and sit down," he said with more authority than he'd displayed since he entered Room 24.

To my astonishment, the kids actually began righting the desks and sorting out their belongings.

Later I would figure out the kids in Room 24 only *appeared* to obey Mr. Schaffer occasionally to lull him into a false sense of security. They wanted him to be off guard when they pulled their next stunt.

Mr. Schaffer didn't know this now. He probably thought the party was over and he could get down to the business of teaching.

"That's better," he said, pleased. "Now I'll take attendance."

"You don't have to do that. We're all here," spoke up a beige-looking boy. He had beige-colored hair, like shredded wheat, and beige-colored eyes. He wasn't a kid you would glance at twice. I knew his name, but he was so boring, I could never remember it.

"Not that I don't take your word for it," Mr. Schaffer said, trying to show the kids he was an all-right guy. He couldn't seem to find his attendance book, though, or his briefcase. The two items he'd walked in with had disappeared. He searched fruitlessly for a few seconds before saying, still in good humor, "Okay, who's the wise guy?"

"WE ALL ARE!" the boys chorused. They cackled and slapped palms.

The culprit wasn't one of the boys, though. A girl with short auburn hair went up to Mr. Schaffer's desk, dangling the missing case and attendance book. Her name was Ginger Green. "Looking for these?"

"Thank you—" Mr. Schaffer began.

"It'll cost you. A quarter apiece." Ginger put the briefcase and book on Mr. Schaffer's desk and sat on them, refusing to surrender his property until he paid up.

Mr. Schaffer dug two quarters out of his pocket. "You kids drive a hard bargain. *Now* we can take attendance." His good humor was wearing a little thin. From his case he took out the attendance book and opened it. "Jason Cruikshank."

"Yo." Jason was short, dark-haired, and cute except for the smirk on his face.

"James Cruikshank."

"Here." The tall, thin boy next to him waved his hand. Their smirks were similar.

Mr. Schaffer peered at them over his reading glasses. "Brothers?"

"Eye-dentical twin cousins," said James. They didn't look a thing alike, except for their smirks. I knew they were brothers, but Mr. Schaffer didn't seem to suspect anything wrong.

"Very unusual," he murmured, fumbling with the loose change in his pocket. A coin fell to the floor with a ringing clink. "James, would you pick that up? You can keep it."

The boy who claimed to be Jason Cruikshank bounded out of his seat so fast, he left tread marks all over his "identical twin cousin."

"So *you're* James," Mr. Schaffer stated. "And you"—he pointed to the one who'd called himself James—"are Jason."

The "twins" grinned sheepishly at being found out.

"They're brothers," the blond boy with the big mouth verified. "James ought to be in seventh grade, but he got left back. Jason is here because James is."

"I want to get left back, too," Jason put in.

"A worthy goal and one I'm sure you'll make." Mr. Schaffer continued the roll call. "Ginger Green."

"Yeah." This was the girl who had conned fifty cents from the teacher. She caught me staring at her and made a face at me.

"Bruce Hall?"

No answer.

"Bruce?" Mr. Schaffer looked around. "Is he here?"

"Yeah, he's here," Jason replied.

"Why doesn't he answer?"

"He's asleep."

Sure enough, the fat red-haired boy was slumped over his desk, seemingly dead to the world. Mr. Schaffer started down the aisle to wake him up.

He shook Bruce's shoulder. "Naptime is over."

Bruce came awake slowly, like a diver surfacing from the depths of the ocean, but the minute Mr. Schaffer turned his back, Bruce launched a spitball that just missed the teacher's ear.

"Robert Moscowitz," Mr. Schaffer called.

Robert, the beige boy, said, "Here."

"You are responsible for the artwork gracing my

blackboard?" Mr. Schaffer asked. A gruesome monster with dripping fangs snarled across the blackboard. The initials *R.M.* were scrawled just below the picture.

"Yeah," Robert admitted with pride. "I drew it."

"You're very good," Mr. Schaffer said. "You should be taking special art classes."

"I am. *This* is my art class."

I was beginning to feel sorry for Mr. Schaffer. It was an uphill battle just to call the roll in this class.

"Rosemary Stern."

"I'm here," came the soft reply.

"Boy, is she *ever* here," snickered James.

Rosemary was the prettiest girl in the class, maybe the whole school. She had long black hair and dark brown eyes. When she smiled, two dimples flashed. On her desk was an array of makeup. She was brushing on purple mascara, squinting into a mirror.

Mr. Schaffer cleared his throat. "Ah, let's put those things away, Rosemary."

"Just let me put on my mascara," Rosemary said amiably.

Mr. Schaffer gave up, probably deciding a beauty parlor in his class was the least of his worries. "Teresa Thompson."

"I'm here." Teresa had streaked hair in a ragged haircut that emphasized her small pointed chin and the enormous chip on her shoulder. "I'm here, but I don't want to be. I hate school more than anything else in the universe. As soon as I'm sixteen, I'm splitting." She slouched in her seat, glaring defiantly at the teacher.

"You might change your mind by then," Mr. Schaffer said.

"No way. I hate school and everything about it. The books are stupid, the homework is stupid, the rules are stupid, the teachers—"

"All right, we get the picture." Mr. Schaffer passed a hand over his forehead. There was only one name he hadn't called.

"Corcoran Wainwright the Third."

Big Mouth lifted one finger, barely. I turned so I could study him better. Aside from his good looks, he had a cool assurance that came from having a fancy name, and the fancy life-style that went with it. He wore expensive designer clothes unselfconsciously. His attitude signaled that he didn't care about money—his parents had plenty. What on earth was he doing in Room 24? I was surprised he wasn't in some prep school. Maybe he'd been thrown *out* of prep school and ended up here.

"Do you go by Corcoran?" Mr. Schaffer inquired.

"My friends call me Corky—" the boy replied.

"Corky, then."

"You're not my friend," Corky said flatly. "I say who my friends are. A teacher can never be my friend."

"All right, Corcoran." Mr. Schaffer drew out the name. "Perhaps by the end of the year you'll see things differently."

"A year!" Corky snorted. "You won't last that long. No teacher ever stays long in this class."

"Is that so?" Mr. Schaffer strode up to the board and erased Robert's creation. With purple chalk he sketched a rough grid on the far section, numbering the squares into a rough calendar. "It's the second week of October. Nearly eleven weeks till Christmas. Not only will I last until Christmas vacation, but you will *beg* me to come back and finish the year with you."

The class responded with hoots and catcalls.

Corky glanced over at me, giving me a confident smile as if to say, That's what *he* thinks. I turned away from him.

Corcoran Wainwright III was clearly the ringleader in Room 24. The kids were all terrible, but Corky had organized them into a gang. I didn't want any part of them.

The bell rang.

"Lunch!" cried Jason. He was out the door before anyone could stop him. The others followed.

Mr. Schaffer, who hadn't yet recovered from calling the roll, pawed through his papers, trying to find our schedule. "Wait!" he called. "It's not your lunch! This class doesn't go to lunch until eleven-forty—"

There was no one left but me.

"I guess I'd better bring them back. I have to show them who's boss," Mr. Schaffer said doubtfully. He stared at the empty classroom. "I don't want to leave you alone here. Why don't you come with me, Austin?"

As we hurried down the hall toward the cafeteria, Mr. Schaffer said, "Maybe I'll let them eat during this lunch period, just this once." He was trying to convince me that *he* made the decision to eat early, but he didn't fool me.

We both knew who was in charge. The Spitball Class lived by their own rules.

Chapter
3

✺ Mrs. Foster, the third-grade teacher who was the cafeteria monitor for the day, got upset when the inmates of Room 24 barreled into the lunchroom. Mr. Schaffer and I were right behind them.

"Are these your students?" Mrs. Foster asked him.

"Yes, I'm Doug Schaffer—" But there was no time for introductions. Corky and Jason and James were cutting in front of the little kids moving through the lunch line. Bruce snatched one kid's tray, too lazy to fetch his own.

"Hey!" squawked the outraged little boy. "That's mine!"

"Tough." Bruce pushed past him.

"We were here first!" another kid protested.

"So sue us." James rudely elbowed the boy out of the way.

The clods from Room 24 acted like overgrown first graders—only real first graders behaved better.

"My class!" Mr. Schaffer ordered. "James, Jason, Bruce—all of you, over here. Right now!"

They paid no attention. Mr. Schaffer headed angrily for the serving line.

Someone must have summoned the principal. Mr. Wren entered the cafeteria and saw what was going on.

"All right," he said firmly. "Fun's over. Back to your room. On the double."

Amazingly, Corky and the others abandoned their trays and swaggered out of the cafeteria.

Mr. Schaffer hurried over to the principal. "I'm sorry for the disruption. They pulled a fast one on me. It won't happen again."

The principal just shook his head. He probably didn't believe Mr. Schaffer. "I'll let you discipline them this time," he said. "You don't need your authority undermined your first day." He went over to speak to the first graders who had been pushed out of line, trying to make them feel better.

Mr. Wren undoubtedly saw the students from Room 24 more times a week than he could count. The little kids' feelings were ruffled, but nobody had gotten hurt. I guess he decided not to put the Room 24 kids on detention.

Mr. Schaffer's shoulders drooped as he moved toward me. "Let's go back to the class," he said. "Before they tear the place down."

The kids were actually sitting at their desks, industriously reading or writing. As I passed Robert's desk, I noticed he was drawing another grisly monster. This one suspiciously resembled the teacher. The book Corky was pretending to read was upside-down. He gave me a little smile.

Mr. Schaffer was cool, though. Any other teacher would have blown his top, but Mr. Schaffer calmly wrote everyone's name except mine on the board and announced, "If your name is up here, you will write a two-hundred-word essay on the importance of following rules. Due tomorrow. There will not be a repeat of today's adventure."

The others in the class sat perfectly still, as if stunned because the teacher hadn't yelled at them. Mr. Schaffer stared back at them, not saying a word.

The bell interrupted the silence. Lunchtime, our *real* lunchtime. The kids took off like escaped convicts.

Erin and Patty were supposed to save me a seat at their table. I figured I had to spend my days in Room 24, but not my lunch periods.

I found my friends sitting with a girl I didn't know. The girl had long honey-colored hair that fell in smooth waves from a black suede hairband. I put my hand up to my own hair. It was probably a mess from running up and down the halls.

Patty jumped up when she saw me. "Austin!" she shrieked, giving me a hug. "It's terrible! Erin told me about your room assignment."

"You mean my jail sentence," I corrected.

The girl with the long hair glanced at me as I sagged wearily into an empty chair.

"Bailey, you know Austin," Patty said.

"No. I don't," Bailey said.

"You guys really don't know each other?" Patty looked from me to Bailey. "Bailey moved into your old house, Austin."

I stared at the blond girl. "Really? You live at Nine-One-Oh-Nine Sudley?"

"Yes."

I had never met the family who bought our house, but I remembered Mom saying they had a daughter about my age. It felt strange, talking to someone who probably had my old room.

"How do you like living in our house?" I asked her.

"It's *our* house now." She took a bite of her sandwich. "I had to paint my room. Those pink walls were boring. It looks *much* better now."

Erin said quickly, "Bailey fixed up your—I mean, her—room really cool. She had a slumber party there a few weeks ago."

"Bailey's the class vice-president," Patty added.

I looked at Bailey Hoffman with envy. She was living my life! Not only did she have my old room, she also had the class office I'd planned to have.

"Aren't you going to eat?" Erin asked me.

I shook my head. I had lost my appetite.

When lunch was over, I went straight to the main office.

"Has anybody left yet?" I asked Mrs. Hopkins, hanging breathlessly over the counter. "You said if somebody left, I could transfer into another room."

"Nope, sorry. It's been a slack morning for drop-outs." Noting my gloomy expression, she said, "Austin, the *second* there is an opening, I'll let you know."

I really didn't deserve to be in that room. I've never been a behavior problem in my life. I always turned in my homework on time, neatly copied over with no eraser holes. Whenever the teacher left the room, the kid who was supposed to take names never had to write my name on the board. So why was this happening to me?

I had to give Mr. Schaffer credit. He actually attempted to teach that afternoon, despite Rosemary's beauty parlor, Bruce's snores, and the textbooks that thumped to the floor one after the other.

"We have an assembly in a few minutes," he announced, glancing anxiously at the clock. "When it's over, you'll go directly to your buses." He was probably relieved not to have to deal with Room 24 the rest of the day.

"Oh, boy," Corky said with exaggerated innocence. "We *love* assemblies, don't we, guys? We've been waiting for this one all week." That remark should have put Mr. Schaffer on guard, but I guess he was worn down.

Absently, as if he were talking to any other class,

he instructed us to line up when the bell rang and walk down to the auditorium single file. There was to be no talking during the assembly. We were to use our best Freeman manners. Personally, I thought he was asking too much, but it wasn't my place to say anything.

The bell jangled and the class charged to the door like stampeding buffalo. Mr. Schaffer couldn't have caught them in a 747. So much for lining up and walking down in an orderly manner.

By the time I reached the auditorium, other classes were already filling the front rows. Instead of filling the next empty row, my class scattered all over the auditorium, claiming the seats on either side of theirs so no one could sit next to them.

"Oh, no," I heard a fifth grade teacher moan to another teacher. "Those kids! Where is their teacher?"

"Right here." Mr. Schaffer panted down the aisle. "Robert, Ginger, Jason, down front." Frantically he rounded up his students. "Fill the row where Austin is sitting."

Once again I was Mr. Schaffer's decoy. He seemed to believe that if the other kids saw me acting normal, they'd copy me. The others came over eventually, but only because they got tired of their game.

Corky sat beside me. "I didn't see you at lunch."

"I wasn't hungry." I stared straight ahead at the stage.

"You lie," he said bluntly. "You're too good to sit

31

with us, aren't you? Goody-goody little Austin hates being stuck with the bad kids."

"I *do* hate it," I returned. "You guys think you're so cool, but you're not. You're stupid, that's what you are."

"You think we're stupid? Let me clue you in. This school dumps on us. They say we're 'discipline problems,' but really we're the garbage heap. Nobody cares about us. You wait. Your so-called friends will start dumping on you, too, just because you're in our class."

"My friends are loyal," I informed him. "They'll stick by me. At the end of the year we'll go on to junior high, but you will still be in Room Twenty-four. You'll probably be left back until you're sixty years old!"

Corky gave a barking laugh. "We probably will, but the funny thing is, you'll be right there with us."

"In your dreams," I retorted.

Two seats down Teresa shot me a black look. I think she was jealous because Corky was talking to me. I glared back at her. Corky made me furious—I wasn't afraid of her or anybody else at that moment.

Mr. Wren climbed the stage steps and asked for our attention.

"Here!" yelled Robert Moscowitz. Everyone in our class but me laughed like hyenas.

With so many kids in the auditorium, the principal couldn't single out who had made the crack, but he frowned in our direction. Then he introduced the guest speaker, a man who was going to help us make our school a Drug Free Zone.

Corky reached under his seat, where he had stored his knapsack. He opened the Velcro flaps unnecessarily slowly. The *riiiiippp* sound went on and on. From the knapsack he pulled out five cans of soda and a bag of crunchy Cheez Doodles.

He passed four of the cans down our row for the others to split, then gave the last soda to me. "We'll have to share. I couldn't fit more than five in my knapsack."

I handed the drink back to him. "I'm not thirsty."

"Suit yourself." He shrugged, tearing open the bag with maximum cellophane crinkle. "I always like a little afternoon snack myself. Cheez Doodle?"

"No, thank you."

The kids around us nudged one another, eyeing the Cheez Doodles and sodas hungrily.

"Hey," the boy behind Corky said. "We want some, too."

Corky didn't even turn around. "Bring your own next time." He passed the bag to the kids in our class but not to anyone else. Jason crammed a whole handful of Cheez Doodles in his mouth all at once. Not an inspiring sight.

I tried to listen to the speaker. It wasn't easy. On a signal from Corky the others rolled their empty soft drink cans under the seats so they clattered down to the front. Then Corky began coughing, a long, racking

33

cough that sounded as if he had a fishbone caught in his throat. The other kids copied, with fake gagging or throwing-up noises. Our row sounded like a hospital ward.

"Shhhh!" I warned, but it was too late.

Mr. Wren launched himself at our row. "Out," he ordered, jerking his head toward the exit. "Come on, move it."

Corky got up with a triumphant smile. His sole intent had been to interrupt the assembly, and he had accomplished it.

"All of you." Mr. Wren's face was like a thundercloud.

The others filed insolently past me. Teresa bumped my leg with her knee, on purpose.

"You, too," Mr. Wren said.

I looked around, feeling like the cheese in that little kids' game, the farmer in the dell. I stood, or rather sat, alone.

I pointed to myself unbelievingly. "You don't mean *me?*"

"Yes, you. Everyone in the class, out."

"But I didn't do anything!" I protested. "I was just sitting here."

"You're in Room Twenty-four, aren't you?"

I nodded miserably.

"Back to your room. Your teacher will deal with you."

Arguing with the principal was suicidal. With every

eye in the entire auditorium on me, I stumbled down the aisle and out the exit.

Corky and the others were fooling around in the hall.

"Were you giving Wren a hard time?" he wanted to know, his eyes sparkling with excitement. Apparently he loved nothing better than trouble.

"No," I said, blinking back tears. If the kids in the Spitball Class saw me crying, they'd hang me by my thumbs. "He was giving *me* a hard time. And it's all your fault!"

"My fault?"

"Yes! Mr. Wren blamed the whole class for what you started, Corcoran Wainwright!"

"You forgot the Third," he said. "I told you Room Twenty-four gets dumped on by this school. They always blame us for everything."

This made no sense to me. Who were "they"? The entire school? "But *you* guys were the ones who acted up," I said. "Why should I take the rap for what you did?"

He grinned carelessly. "That's life! Better get used to it, Austin."

The final bell of the day rang. The kids in Room 24 vanished as if by magic. I made a beeline for my bus.

On the bus I spotted Chester sitting with a couple of third grade boys. He'd made friends already.

Then I saw Bailey Hoffman. Of course she'd ride

our bus. She lived in our old house, which was near the neighborhood we lived in now.

There was room next to her on the seat. It would be nice to have a bus friend. After all, we had a lot in common. The same bedroom, the same friends.

"Hi," I said.

"Hello." She spoke without enthusiasm. "Weren't you one of *those kids* kicked out of the assembly?"

"Yeah, but it was a mix-up. Mr. Wren tossed the whole class out, even though I wasn't doing anything."

She sniffed, unconvinced.

I wanted to change the subject. Also, I wanted to sit down. After a long day in Room 24, I was tired. "Is anyone sitting here?" I asked.

Bailey slid her knapsack from her lap to the empty part of the seat. "Yes, somebody is."

I knew good and well nobody was, but there was no point in making a fuss. She didn't want me to sit beside her because I was one of *those kids*. I'd spent only one day in Room 24, but already the curse was following me.

Chapter
4

✿ "I had a great day!" Chester chirped as we got off the bus in front of the Lake Ridge sign. The sign showed a sailboat scooting along waves. There wasn't a lake within ten miles. Talk about optimism.

"I'm glad somebody did," I said sarcastically. "I hate my class. Neither of my friends is in my room." Of course they weren't. They'd have to be on the FBI's Most-Wanted list to land in the Spitball Class, or else be the unluckiest person in the universe, like me.

"I didn't know anybody in my class, either," Chester said cheerfully. "Except two yucky girls. I made all new friends."

Life was so much simpler for an eight-year-old. I almost wished I were back in third grade again.

My knapsack felt like it was loaded with boulders. I slid it off my shoulder and let it drag up the steps of our townhouse. I couldn't have been more tired if I'd spent the day busting rocks in a labor camp.

Mom met us at the door. "Hi, kids. How was the first day back at your old school?" She led the way past cartons and chairs piled with clothes.

With his usual boundless energy, Chester skipped into the hall, tossed his knapsack on an unpacked box near the door, babbling, "Guess what? I made four new friends, and my teacher is real nice."

"Sounds like you had a good day," Mom said to him.

I followed my mother and Chester into the kitchen. Here, at least, everything was in order. Not only were all our dishes and pans unpacked, but the refrigerator and cupboards were stocked. Mom had found time to go to the store. A plate of store-bought brownies sat on the counter. Chester saw them the same time I did and fell on them as if he were starving.

Mom watched me drop my knapsack into the nearest chair.

"How was your day, Austin?" she asked. "It should have been old home week for you and Erin and Patty."

It *should* have been, but it wasn't. More like a horror show.

When I didn't answer right off, Mom said, a note of concern in her voice, "I know it's been hard on you two—changing schools twice in such a short time and moving—"

38

"Austin was the one who wanted to move," Chester said accusingly. He looked at Mom as he crammed a whole brownie in his mouth. He sensed Mom's worry over my silence and wanted to call attention to himself again.

"Chester, smaller bites, please. Austin, I wish you'd say something. You look like you lost your best friend. What happened today?"

"Well . . ." I hedged.

My brother was right. I *was* the one who wanted to move back to Virginia. It was no secret I hated every minute we were in Orlando. According to Mom, I complained from the time I opened my eyes in the morning until I went to bed at night.

On the drive north this past weekend, I sang and laughed and even let Chester play with the pegboard IQ test on our table in the restaurant we stopped at for dinner. When we crossed the state line into Virginia, I cheered.

So how could I possibly be miserable? What excuse did I have to complain now? Would anyone understand?

"Austin!"

"Sorry, Mom," I said. "I was just—noticing how neat the kitchen is. You've worked hard today."

"Yes, I have. Now, how about *your* day. You *did* go to school, didn't you?"

"Yeah. It was okay," I lied. "I don't know anybody in my class." I left out the fact I had been put into the notorious Spitball Class. I didn't even want Chester to know. The little kids' classes were on the other side of the building, and by some miracle Chester hadn't seen me in the cafeteria earlier, when Room 24 tried to take over the little kids' lunch shift.

"You're not in Erin's class?" Mom asked. "Or Patty's?" She handed me a brownie and a glass of milk.

I shook my head. "They're in T and G. Talented and Gifted," I spelled out.

"You'll never be in *that* class," Chester said.

"Chester, be still." To me, Mom added, "Well, you'll see your friends after school, and you can make new friends. You and Erin and Patty were a bit too thick, I always thought."

I didn't *want* to make friends with those awful kids. And the feeling was mutual. "I think I'll go over to Erin's," I said, finishing my snack. "Is the phone hooked up yet?"

"Yes."

After locating the telephone under a pile of sheets, I dialed Erin's number. We used to pop in and out of each other's houses all the time, but since I'd been away for a while, I figured it would be nicer to call first.

Erin answered on the second ring. "Bailey?" she said.

"No," I said. "It's me. Austin. Austin *Sommers?*" I added when Erin didn't answer right away.

"*Aus*tin! I saw you in the assembly. You got kicked out! I bet it was awful."

40

"The worst. Can I come over and tell you guys about it? You wouldn't believe what this class is like. I can't believe it myself. You know it wasn't my fault I got thrown out of the assembly. I was just sitting there and—"

"Patty's coming over as soon as band practice is over," Erin broke in.

"Good! I can't wait to see you both. It'll be our first real visit since I got back from Florida. We can play Monopoly like we used to."

Our Monopoly games were legendary. They'd last for days. We'd leave the board set up in Erin's room while we watched old movies.

"I don't know where the Monopoly set is," Erin said. "Mom packed it away. Besides, we're kind of old for it."

We were? We weren't too old a couple of months ago. "Oh," I said. "Can I still come over?" Why did I have a funny, squishy feeling in the hollow of my stomach?

"That'd be okay . . ." Erin said hesitantly. I waited for the *but* I knew would follow. "But Patty and I have to do math and science. We have *tons* of homework in T and G. Bailey'll be here any minute to help us. She's a whiz in math."

My heart dropped into the squishy pit that was my stomach. "Is Bailey Hoffman in your class, too?"

"Yeah," Erin replied. "She's the smartest one."

Of course Bailey would be in the Talented and

41

Gifted class. Was there anything the great Bailey Hoffman couldn't do, except be nice to me?

Listening to Erin rattle on about the neat stuff they were doing in T and G, I felt more untalented and ungifted by the minute. I couldn't play a musical instrument like Patty, and I definitely wasn't a brain like Erin or Bailey.

"You understand, don't you?" Erin was saying. "If we didn't have all this homework ... Maybe you can come over tomorrow. Oh, wait, I just remembered Bailey and I have a class meeting. How about Thursday?"

"I might be busy," I heard myself answering. Doing what, I had no idea.

"Oh." Erin sounded mildly disappointed. "Well, whenever. Patty and Bailey just came in. Got to run. Bye!"

"Save me a seat at lunch tomorrow!" I managed to squeeze in before she hung up.

I never had to ask them to save me a seat before. After all, we'd been best friends for years. Things were different now, though. I'd only been gone for two months, but it seemed like a million years.

Maybe, I thought, Erin and Patty figured I didn't like Bailey. We *did* get off on the wrong foot. Maybe I misunderstood Bailey's unfriendly signals. Maybe she was just shy.

I would patch things up tomorrow, I told myself. I'd be super-nice to Bailey. Erin and Patty would see that the three of us belonged together, no matter what class we were in.

I was in a good mood when I walked into Room 24 the next morning until the noise smacked me in the face like a wet washrag. Then my good mood evaporated.

Mr. Schaffer hadn't arrived yet and probably wouldn't, if he had a shred of sense left. Unable to tell if the kids were rejoicing Mr. Schaffer's resignation or just being their natural wild selves, I sat down at my desk.

The principal came on the PA system with morning announcements, but I couldn't hear a word he said. Were we going to have a teacher today? I wondered. Either Mr. Wren decided to leave us teacherless, on the outside chance we'd kill one another and his Room 24 problem would vanish, or else he couldn't pay anyone enough to take this class.

Corky came in then and slapped my desk. "Told you he wouldn't last. I hope the next one is a lady. They're easy to make cry."

I glared at him. "You ought to be ashamed. Mr. Schaffer was a nice man. I hope he gets a better class than *this* one."

At that moment Mr. Schaffer strode in, briefcase swinging. "Good morning, class," he greeted. "Sorry I'm late. I was detained. I had to call a mechanic." He looked pointedly at Corky, whose face was a mask of innocence, but didn't tell us what was wrong with his car. Whatever Corky did, it must have been awful. I was amazed Mr. S. bothered coming back to this class.

"You got car trouble?" Jason asked. "Me and James will fix it, and we won't charge you much." He and his brother headed for the door.

"Sit down, boys," Mr. Schaffer said. "We've already wasted enough time." He pulled out the roll book and began checking off names. "All here, I see. Now, let's get started. Pass your essays forward, please." No one moved. "The essay you were supposed to write about not breaking rules?" Giving up, he sighed and pointed to Ginger. "Tell me where you are in math."

"What?"

"I said, tell me where you are in math," he repeated patiently, as if explaining to a two-year-old. "In your textbook. What page are you on?"

"Oh. Where are we in that book?" she asked Bruce.

Bruce held up a tattered math book by one corner. Most of the pages had been ripped out. The rest were covered with drawings. "This book, you mean?"

"Yeah," Ginger replied.

Bruce made a great show of leafing through the ragged pages that were left. His finger stabbed a page. "Here."

Ginger carried the book to Mr. Schaffer. "This is as far as we got."

Mr. Schaffer raised his eyebrows. "The introduc-

44

tion? Today, I'd like to get a little farther than that. Do you all have books?"

Dumb question.

"Mine's in the toilet," Jason said.

"I left mine at my other school," Teresa said.

"Re*form* school," James joked.

"All right!" Mr. Schaffer held up a hand. "I'll put problems on the board." He vigorously erased Robert's latest masterpiece—a warty portrait of Mr. Wren—then wrote some problems. He asked Rosemary and Robert to go up to the board.

Rosemary picked up a piece of chalk and began making very faint markings beneath her problem.

"Press down," Mr. Schaffer said. "We can't read your answer."

She turned. "I don't know how to do it."

Mr. Schaffer went through the steps of the problem while Rosemary studied the design of his tie. When he asked her if she understood, she nodded, but I could tell his explanation had flown in one ear and out the other.

"What is that?" Mr. Schaffer asked Robert.

"What's what? Oh, *that.*" Beneath his problem, Robert had doodled a horizontal line with a bump in the middle. "It's a snake that got run over."

The class broke up. Corky laughed the loudest.

Mr. Schaffer said, "Corcoran, I think you ought to go see the principal." He must have caught on that Corky was the class ringleader.

"I can't."

"What do you mean, you can't?"

Corky fixed him with his light blue eyes. "I'm not supposed to go to the office more than once a day, Mr. Wren says. It's his rule, man, not mine. And I've already seen him once today."

That explained why Corky was late.

Mr. Schaffer folded his arms. He seemed very interested. "And what were you in trouble for, first thing?"

"Some kid said he saw me fooling around in the parking lot." Corky's tone implied there wasn't a grain of truth in the accusation.

"Isn't that a coincidence? Someone let the air out of *my* tires. I will check with Mr. Wren about his so-called rule. In the meantime, stop disrupting. The rest of the class is trying to learn something."

"We are?" James quipped.

With a heavy sigh Mr. Schaffer pulled out his chair. He hadn't sat down since he came in. Reaching down, he picked up an object and held it delicately between two fingers. It was a mousetrap.

"No flies on you guys," he said.

"I think the cafeteria ladies stay awake at night thinking up revolting things to feed us," I said, making light conversation as I poked a fork at my lunch, a barbeque rib sandwich.

"I don't buy lunch anymore," Erin stated, crunching a carrot stick. "My mother says school lunches have too much fat."

46

"What *is* that?" said Shawn Zuskin, pointing at my sandwich. "Squirrel ribs?"

"I hate those urine cups they put vegetables in," Bailey contributed, just as I put a forkful of corn in my mouth.

The tiny paper cup *did* look like the kind in doctors' offices and that caused my appetite to nosedive.

Erin and Patty had saved me a seat, but it was with the T and G kids. They all brought their lunches, healthy stuff like zucchini bread. Shawn and the others seemed okay, but Bailey Hoffman barely said hello. She gave Erin a look that clearly said, You're letting one of *those kids* sit with us?

The inmates in Room 24 sat clustered together at a table near the trash cans. Corky watched me as I steered my tray away from their table and headed for the T and G table. He and the others would probably razz me to death about being too good to sit with them, but I desperately needed to be with my friends.

"Erin," I said now. "What are you doing this weekend?"

"I don't know." She finger-combed her dark hair, a gesture she always made when she was nervous. "Why?"

"I thought we'd get together. Maybe go to the mall like we used to?" I suggested, reminding her of the great times we had.

Patty explained to Bailey, "Austin hung out with us last year." The way she said "last year" made it sound as if that was all in the past.

47

"You come with us," I offered, recalling my vow to be nicer to Bailey. "I haven't been to the mall since I moved back from Florida. I could use a break from the Spitball Class."

Shawn stared at me. "Are you really in that class?"

"It's a mistake," I said hastily. "A horrible mistake. As soon as they find room for me in another class, I'm out of that dump. It won't be a minute too soon, either."

Shawn and Bailey exchanged a doubtful glance across the table. It was obvious they didn't believe me. They thought I truly *belonged* in Room 24. Erin and Patty didn't exactly rush to my defense.

"I guess you're in that room for a good reason," Shawn said, before changing the subject.

More than half of my lunch was still on my plate, but I couldn't force down another bite. I would never shed the label that came with being in Room 24. Even if I made straight A's, volunteered to scrub the lunch tables, and sang the lead in the class winter musical, it still wouldn't make any difference.

As long as I was in the Spitball Class, I was one of *them*.

Chapter
5

❋ I managed to corner Erin by the garbage cans when she went to throw away her trash. "You know it's not my fault I'm in that class. How come you didn't say anything to back me up?"

"I know it's not your fault," she said, but she didn't act sorry.

I grabbed her arm, forcing her to meet my eyes. "Have I changed?" I demanded. "I'm the same person I was when I left last summer, aren't I?"

"Sure you are."

"So how come you're treating me like something you scrape off your shoe?"

Erin was staring over my shoulder. "I think that kid wants you." Slipping out of my grasp, she hurried back to her table.

Corky Wainwright was signaling from the Spitball

table. "Hey, Austin, how come you don't sit with us? You'd have more fun over here."

"Because she's too good, that's why," Teresa said scornfully. "She'd rather be dumped on by the brainy crowd than sit with us."

Her words struck so close to the truth that tears stung my eyes. That was exactly what the T and G group was doing, dumping on me. Yet I acted eager for any crumbs they might fling my way. Disgusted with myself, I tossed my disposable lunch tray at the trash can. It missed and landed on the floor, but I didn't stop to pick it up. I ran from the cafeteria, even though the bell wouldn't ring for another five minutes.

There wasn't any place to run to, I discovered, except my classroom. Mr. Schaffer was working at his desk, his shirtsleeves rolled up.

"Austin," he said. "Is something wrong?"

Only everything, I felt like answering. "Have you heard about my transfer?" I asked hopefully. "I saw you in the office earlier. Did Miss Hopkins tell you somebody had left?"

"No. Listen, Austin." He sat back. "I know you're anxious to get out of this class. I don't blame you. But I'm glad you're in here. You give the kids an example to follow besides Corky's. That boy has a quick mind, but his ideas aren't quite in line with mine," he added with a wry smile. "If this class would work together, we might make it."

In the empty classroom Mr. Schaffer's reasoning made perfect sense. Yet as soon as the kids came surging back, reason flew out the window. Logic might not work in Room 24, but at least Mr. Schaffer was trying.

It took him the better part of the afternoon just to explain our homework. There were endless trips to the rest rooms and the water fountain. Jason mashed James's finger in the pencil sharpener, and James had to go to the clinic. A few minutes before the last bell, Mr. Schaffer managed to snag everyone's attention.

"Tomorrow," he said uncertainly, as if he doubted the sun would ever rise again, "I would like you to turn in a one-page essay on how you might save the environment. In ink."

"Does spelling count?" Robert asked. "How do you spell *environment?*"

"How do you spell *dumbhead?*" said Bruce.

"What was the topic again?" Ginger wanted to know.

Mr. Schaffer rephrased the assignment. "What would you do to improve the environment?"

"I'd tear down all the schools," Teresa declared. "And put up frozen yogurt stands."

Erin called me that night. I had just finished copying over my environment essay.

"I'm sorry about today," she said.

"You are?" I was so surprised by her apology I couldn't think of anything to say.

"Patty and I were talking," she went on. "We really haven't had a chance to get together since you moved back. Can you come to the mall Saturday?"

I let out the breath I'd been holding. "I think so. Mom's not here, but I'm pretty sure she'll say it's okay."

"Great! About one, by the clock?" That was our old meeting place.

"It'll be like old times again," I said. Erin agreed.

We yakked a few minutes, then hung up. I forgot to ask if Bailey Hoffman was coming, too. Probably not. It wouldn't be like old times if a new girl was along.

The next morning I turned in my environment essay. It was exactly one page, in ink. My suggestion was to put recycling centers at all the supermarkets. People always had to go to the grocery store, but they didn't always make special trips to the recycling centers.

Mr. Schaffer acted surprised when I was the only one to turn in a paper. He shouldn't have been. *I* wasn't.

"Well," he said, sounding extremely disappointed. "I thought this was a topic you'd be excited about. You should take an interest in the world you live in."

"Wait—" Corky said. "I did my homework."

"Why didn't you pass your paper in when I asked for it?"

"I didn't write a paper. I did a project." Corky went

up to Mr. Schaffer's desk, carrying a gym bag. "It's in here." The sides of the gym bag bulged mysteriously. Something was in there, alive.

"Why am I suspicious? Okay, show us what you brought. And it had better have something to do with the environment."

"It does." Setting the bag on the teacher's desk, Corky unzipped it. A strange sound, like a yowl, filled the room.

We all leaned forward, curious to see Corky's "project."

A gray and white cat shot out of the bag like a rocket. It leapt over the desk and landed on Mr. Schaffer's shoulder.

"Yeow!" he cried.

Corky pulled the cat off Mr. Schaffer, but not before the cat dug his claws in good. "Are you okay?" he asked, concerned.

Mr. Schaffer checked for blood. "I guess I'll live."

"I was asking Ringo. Are you okay, cat? He was cooped up in that bag a long time."

"It's a wonder he didn't suffocate. Phewww!" Robert pretended to swoon over his desk.

"I had the zipper unzipped a little," Corky said. "He could breathe."

Mr. Schaffer was angry. "Corcoran, you know the rules. Animals aren't allowed in the building unless for a specific project."

"He *is* for a specific project."

"You did not get permission from the office," Mr. Schaffer argued. "And what does this cat have to do with the environment?"

"Animal rights," Corky replied smoothly. "Animals are part of our world, only they don't get to do the things we do. So I brought Ringo to school. Cats should be able to go to school, don't you think?"

Mr. Schaffer rubbed his shoulder. "Ringo wants to be here about as much as the rest of you do."

"Then this is the perfect class for him." Corky petted his cat. I could hear Ringo's rumbling purr all the way where I was sitting.

Corky was sent to the office to call his mother to come get Ringo. By the time the excitement had died down, it was time for lunch. I couldn't wait to tell my lunch group about the morning. As I told the story, everyone listened intently.

"When Corky pulled the cat off the teacher, I thought he was going to rip Mr. Schaffer's arm off. The cat, I mean, not Corky." I laughed, scooping the last few peas from the specimen cup on my lunch tray.

"You mean he brought a live animal to school in a *gym bag?*" Shawn Zuskin asked.

"Yeah. It was hysterical. I've never seen a cat move so fast. *Wsshhht!* Like a firecracker." I demonstrated with my fork, still laughing.

Bailey frowned. "I don't think that's funny."

"It wasn't *funny,* about the cat," I said, backpedaling. "Well, yes, it was. You had to be there."

"*That* will never happen."

Bailey had a way of ending conversations. Ever since I started eating lunch with Erin and Patty's new friend, I was always being cut off by her. She was forever putting me down.

It was hard to like her. On the bus she hogged a whole seat to herself and barely said hello to me. That morning she had put her feet up on the empty part of her seat, showing off her red leather boots.

Instead of constantly hoping that Miss Hopkins would tell me I'd been transferred to a regular classroom, I began wishing that *Bailey* would be sent to do time in Room 24 so I could take her place in the T and G group.

Patty sided with Bailey. "I don't think it was funny, either. Somebody ought to report that Corky kid for cruelty to animals."

Erin nodded her agreement. "Poor cat."

"For heaven's sake," I exploded. "The *teacher* was there. Corky got in trouble! Are you happy?" Suddenly my funny story had become an issue. I didn't feel like talking anymore.

No one noticed. The others began discussing their summer reading projects, trying to determine who had read the most books. I sat like a lump over my cold tuna casserole, invisible.

Mr. Schaffer wasn't the only gullible person in Room 24. Just as he shouldn't have been surprised when no one but me wrote the essay for homework,

I shouldn't have been floored when Erin called me Friday night to tell me she and Patty couldn't make it to the mall the next day. They had lame excuses. Erin "suddenly remembered" a dentist appointment. Patty had clarinet practice. I wondered if Bailey Hoffman had anything to do with this.

I was quiet at breakfast Saturday morning. Mom decided it was "girl's day out" and took me to the mall for lunch. Then we did some shopping, but for once I didn't feel like shopping for clothes. While Mom was trying on outfits, I wandered around the upper level of the mall. I always enjoyed looking down at the people on the lower level.

That's where I saw Erin and Patty as they came out of Record World. Bailey Hoffman skipped out a few seconds later, swinging a shopping bag. They were laughing, obviously having a great time.

I watched them for a few minutes, half hoping Erin would look up to see me at the glass rail. I wanted to make a face at her. But she didn't look up. She never sensed my presence. Why should she? She and Patty didn't want me around anymore. I might as well still be in Florida, or on the moon.

Bailey Hoffman had taken my place.

"Sorry, Austin," Miss Hopkins said before I could ask.

I stopped by the office so often, the secretary knew what I wanted. Our conversations were reduced to a sort of Morse code.

"Any word?" I asked, meaning any news about my transfer, and she'd say, "Nope," meaning nobody had moved or dropped out. Still, I kept hoping.

To delay going into Room 24 as long as I could, I went into the girls' room to fix my hair. In the mirror I could see the three stalls behind me. The red boots under the closed door of the middle stall looked familiar.

Teresa and Ginger burst in, both carrying books. Right away I knew they were up to something. The inmates of the Spitball Class never used books for anything but weapons.

"Does my hair look okay?" Teresa said in an overly sweet voice.

"Perfect," Ginger replied, giggling hysterically.

I put my brush in my purse, getting ready to leave. Whatever they were up to, I didn't want any part of it.

Teresa put her finger to her lips and tiptoed over to the stalls. Silent as a cat burglar, she jammed the cover of a geography book into the crack between the door and the slide-lock of the middle door.

The bell rang. Teresa and Ginger breezed out. "Don't be late, Austin!" Teresa sang over her shoulder.

A toilet flushed. The person inside the middle stall tried to open the jammed door.

"Hey! This door is stuck!" an indignant voice yelled.

I walked over to the stalls. All I had to do was pull the book away and the girl would be free.

"Is anybody out there?" the voice bellowed. "As soon as I get out of here, I'm going to Mr. Wren! You'll get detention till you're thirty!"

The voice belonged to Bailey Hoffman, owner of the red boots and lousy disposition.

"Unlock this door! Do you hear me?"

The late bell rang. Not wanting to be late to class, I walked out. Somebody would come along and rescue her—sooner or later. I hoped it would be much, much later.

Erin rushed up to me in the lunch line. "I have to talk to you," she said urgently.

I reached for the specimen cup of fruit cocktail. I had decided never to speak to Erin or Patty again, but now I changed my mind. Erin wanted to talk to me! Maybe she and Patty finally realized they'd rather have me for a friend than Bailey Hoffman. They probably had a rotten time with Bailey at the mall—though they didn't look miserable when I saw them. Still, something must have happened to bring them to their senses.

Erin was waiting for me when I left the serving line with my tray.

"Where do you want to talk?" I asked. "You and me and Patty at our own table, just like old times?"

Erin shook her head.

"Okay," I said agreeably. "We'll go to your table." I was anxious to hear Erin and Patty beg me to come back to their group.

"That's just it," Erin said. "You can't sit at our table anymore. Not after this morning."

"What are you talking about?"

"Bailey's furious at you for locking her in the bathroom."

I nearly dropped my tray. "I never locked her in the bathroom!"

"She heard you. She heard another girl call your name."

I couldn't believe Erin would take Bailey's side before she heard mine. "I was *in* there, but I didn't lock her in. Teresa and Ginger did it. Honestly, Erin. Do you think I go around locking people in bathrooms?"

"How come you didn't let her out?" she accused.

I didn't answer. Any excuse I offered would have revealed how much I resented Bailey.

"Bailey doesn't want you at our table anymore," Erin said.

"Bailey, Bailey, Bailey! Who died and left her queen? What about you? Or Patty? Don't *you* want to sit with me anymore? Or does Bailey do your thinking for you, too?"

"You're in *that* class now," Erin replied, as if that summed up everything. "Sorry, Austin," she added before retreating to her table.

Bailey Hoffman smirked at me. She had won and

she knew it. She had completely turned Erin and Patty against me.

Blinking back tears, I stood in the middle of the cafeteria still holding on to my tray. Everyone was staring at me. I wanted to throw my tray on the floor and run out, but then everyone would know that Austin Sommers had been rejected by her friends.

Someone tugged at my sleeve. It was Corky Wainwright.

"What are you, a street sign?" he asked. "Why don't you quit acting like a snob and sit with us?"

Sit at the Spitball table, where they threw food and popped milk cartons? It was unthinkable. I didn't have any choice in my room assignment, but I could sit where I wanted at lunch.

"Come on," Corky insisted. "Who needs those jerks?"

Glancing back at Erin's table, I saw they were all laughing.

"You're right," I agreed. "Who needs those jerks?" I followed him over to the Spitball table and sat next to Teresa.

She gave me a hard stare. "I thought you were too good to eat over here. Why the sudden change of heart?"

"I just want to eat," I said.

"Truce," Corky told Teresa.

Suddenly I realized he had rescued me from terrible embarrassment. I didn't say thanks.

He flipped my butter pat upside down on my tray. "I couldn't leave you standing in the middle of the floor like a dork. You're one of us."

I looked around at my classmates' faces, some smeared with jelly, one (Jason's) with milk dribbling down his chin. Then I laughed, sputtering apple juice out my nose.

Teresa regarded me thoughtfully. I wondered if she was changing her opinion of me. Then she handed me a napkin and said, as if bestowing a great honor on me, "You can pop the first milk carton."

Chapter
6

❀ Becoming accepted into the Spitball Class, I discovered, was a little like walking off a cliff. It seemed like such a daring, exhilarating thing to do, even if it *was* foolhardy. In midair I decided maybe it wasn't such a hot idea after all, but it was too late. I was headed straight for the bottom.

I thought I would miss having my two best friends, but now I had eight *new* friends, all with records.

When the calendar on the board showed Mr. Schaffer had survived an incredible three and a half weeks, Corky decided to launch a plan he code-named Total Annihilation. He wanted to make Mr. Schaffer quit and was taking ideas from the class.

"We could always plant a bomb in his briefcase," Robert suggested.

"Too messy," Corky said. "What else can we do to his car?"

"Nothing," Jason replied. "He puts that cover on it now."

Mr. Schaffer was no dummy, despite the fact that he continued to come to Room 24 day after day. After James and Jason shave-creamed his car—so thoroughly they told us it took them three hours to clean it off—Mr. Schaffer began parking his car under the principal's window and draping it with a special car cover that tied over the wheels. By rights the Cruikshank brothers should have been expelled or at least gotten a month of detention, but Mr. Schaffer only asked them to clean his car.

"Why don't we forget it?" I said to Corky. "Mr. Schaffer is cool. He's not like most teachers."

"True," Corky admitted. "But he still tries to make us do stuff like math and history."

"So? What's so bad about that?"

Ginger scoffed, "You mean you actually *like* schoolwork?"

"Some of it," I answered truthfully. "At least it's something to do. Just sitting around is boring. Don't you guys ever get bored?"

"Not me," Corky said.

I wasn't surprised. Anyone who could organize a plan called Total Annihilation was probably incapable of boredom. But the others weren't as clever as Corky. I wondered if the reason Bruce slept so much and Rosemary messed with makeup all day was because they were bored.

"Austin is right," Teresa said, suddenly siding with me. "He's not bad for a teacher. Why don't we let him stay?"

"Because," Corky stated. "It's traditional that teachers don't last in our class. Besides, I don't trust him. He's *too* nice. I bet he's up to something."

Just then Mr. Schaffer sailed in, never suspecting he was the object of a plan called Total Annihilation. "Good morning," he said.

After checking to make sure no one had stretched a trip wire across the front of the room, he immediately plunged into a poetry reading. This was *his* latest strategy, to start the day with a cannon-shot lesson. I guess he figured if he took the class by surprise, he might actually get them to swallow a dose of literature. Mr. Schaffer began:

> "I think that I shall never see
> A poem lovely as a tree."

Corky followed with a line about dogs and what they like to do to trees. The class broke up. I laughed, too. Corky was really funny. But I did feel sorry for Mr. Schaffer, who stood looking at us with a hurt expression.

"Okay, maybe Joyce Kilmer is a bad choice." He leafed through his book of poetry.

"Yeah. Forget that broad," James said.

"For your information, Joyce Kilmer was a man."

"No wonder he wrote dumb poems," added Jason, never far behind his brother in the smart-aleck department.

"Let's try Emily Dickinson. Listen to this, class. 'Hope is the thing with feathers . . .' "

Bruce slouched over his desk, making fake snore sounds. Corky tore off bits of paper and began showering them on Bruce's head. We all watched, wondering how much paper Corky could pile on Bruce's head before he caught on. When his head resembled a trash dump, he snorted awake, pawing at his head like a hamster with mites. The class giggled.

" 'Yet, never in the extremity/it asked a crumb of me!' " Mr. Schaffer finished doggedly.

"What a crumb-y poem." Corky yawned. If he'd shut up, the others might actually pay attention.

Mr. Schaffer tried one more time. " 'I'm Nobody! Who are you? Are you—Nobody—too?' "

"I'm not nobody!" Corky interrupted. "I am *some*body."

Mr. Schaffer glanced up, realizing he had struck a nerve for the first time with a lesson. "Of course you're somebody. We are all somebody. Emily Dickinson was somebody, too, though she was very shy and became a recluse—that's someone who avoids people—in her later years. Who would like to read the rest of the poem? It's really very funny."

But that was too much like real work. Led by Corky, the class began punching one another and cracking jokes.

I felt bad for Mr. Schaffer. "I'm listening," I told him, hoping to make him feel better. "The others are listening, too. It's just that—"

Of course, they weren't listening. Mr. Schaffer studied his boisterous class, the book of poetry dangling from his hand. The kids were trying to see who was the loudest, the funniest, the most important. I watched Mr. Schaffer watching them and saw inspiration slowly brighten his glum expression.

Running over to his desk, he swept it bare in one smooth motion. Books, notebooks, lesson plans, and papers all crashed to the floor. Everyone stopped talking and carrying on to gawk in amazement. This was it, they were probably thinking. The teacher was finally throwing in the towel.

But he wasn't. If anything, Mr. Schaffer acted more determined than ever. "Okay, everybody, starting right now—" he proclaimed. "Starting from this *second*, we won't be doing conventional work—"

Cheers and catcalls erupted.

"We can go home!" Robert cried joyfully.

Mr. Schaffer held up his hand for silence, which he got for once. "Not quite. Instead of conventional work, we'll begin a brand-new unit, never done in the history of this class. Project All About Me."

"All about me?" Ginger echoed. "I already know all about me. I was born in Washington, D.C., on July—"

"Save it," Mr. Schaffer interrupted. "Save it for the

66

papers you're going to write—" General groans. "Stop bellyaching. You might find you don't know as much about yourselves as you think you do."

He unlocked the supply closet and grabbed a stack of paper and a fistful of pencils. Jogging up and down the aisles, he gave us each paper and a pencil. Mr. Schaffer caught on fast. If he had said, "Take out paper and a pen," he would have spent the rest of the day hearing excuses and rounding up supplies for everyone. The kids in Room 24 were experts in delay tactics.

"Who would know more about me than me?" Corky asked.

"Oh, you know all kinds of facts, like where you were born and so forth, but you may not be *aware* of yourself as a person," Mr. Schaffer said. "That's what this project is all about. Awareness. It's time you launched yourselves into the world, instead of hiding out in this room."

"We aren't hiding here—they *sent* us here," Corky corrected.

"We'll let that go for now," said Mr. Schaffer.

Bruce loudly sniffed his armpit. "I'm here in this world."

"I'll say." Teresa fanned the air in front of her. "Some people we could do without."

I thought Mr. Schaffer was going to make us keep a journal or something, but instead he said, "I want you to write about the best present you ever got for

Christmas. Any Christmas. Also, the present you wanted most and never got. This paper can be two sentences or a whole page, but you *must write something.* No one goes to lunch until everyone has completed the assignment."

"I don't mind missing lunch." Jason folded his paper into an airplane. "Me and James brought our lunch."

"I don't think you understand. Not only will you miss lunch, but recess, too."

Corky and Robert exchanged smirks. Missing recess was no big deal in Room 24, where recess lasted all day long.

"And," Mr. Schaffer added emphatically, "you'll miss your bus. You won't be allowed to leave this room until I have your papers." He stood resolutely by the door, as if he intended to bar the exit.

"You can't do that," Corky protested. "There's a law."

"You refuse to abide by the school's rules, or laws," Mr. Schaffer returned. "But you'll abide by mine." He went back to his desk and sat down.

Everyone started fooling around.

"One time I got this neat machine gun—" Bruce told Robert.

"Write it down," Mr. Schaffer ordered.

I knew Mr. Schaffer was counting on me, so I headed the paper with my name and date. The first part was easy. A long time ago my mother gave me a jewelry box that had belonged to my grandmother.

When you opened the lid, a tiny ballerina stood up and twirled to the tune of "The Blue Danube."

The music box fascinated me. I used to lift the lid and lower it slowly, wondering where the dancer went when the lid was closed. The ballerina was stiff, and it seemed to me that it would break. I finally discovered the dancer's feet were hinged. The whole figure lay flat when the lid was down.

The second part of the essay was harder. I usually got whatever I asked for, mainly because I didn't ask for outrageous presents like Chester did. My brother scribbled long, detailed letters to Santa asking for real submarines or his own island. My list was sensible—ordinary stuff like clothes or cassettes.

So that's what I put, that I had never been disappointed on Christmas morning. Laying my pencil down, I realized something was wrong. No noise, nobody throwing spitballs, nobody being pushed out the window. Everyone was writing! Anyone walking into Room 24 that moment would have thought this was a regular class.

The shock must have been too much for Mr. Schaffer. He was slumped over his desk. I finally realized he was not having a heart attack, but was scribbling in a notebook, too. "Who's finished?" he asked after a while.

I raised my hand. So did Rosemary, Teresa, and Bruce. Corky slowly raised his hand. The others followed, as if waiting for his signal.

"Wonderful! Now we'll read them in class."

"No fair!" Corky exclaimed. "If we were going to tell it, we wouldn't have had to write it."

"Whoever said life was fair?" Mr. Schaffer said crisply. "Your papers will be graded, but I think it would be nice to share your experiences with your fellow students. Who wants to be first? Austin?"

Naturally he'd pick me, knowing I was the only one who wouldn't give him an argument. I walked to the front of the room self-consciously. Reading a paper to the Spitball Class wasn't like reading to any other class. I should have been wearing a bulletproof vest.

" 'The best Christmas present I ever got was a jewelry box that belonged to my grandmother,' " I began nervously.

Amazingly, the class listened until I got to the second half of my paper.

"Wouldn't you know Austin always got whatever she wanted?" Corky sneered. "Must be nice, having a perfect life."

My face felt hot. "I don't have a perfect life," I said defensively. "Ever since we moved back from Florida, my life has been a mess. My friends have changed—"

"And you're stuck in this class," Corky added.

"Mr. Schaffer," I said. "Can I sit down now?"

"Yes, Austin. Thank you very much. Your essay was very interesting. Now, who's next? James?"

I had trouble concentrating. Mr. Schaffer said my paper was interesting, but he didn't say it was good.

Would I get an A? It wasn't my fault I never asked for things I knew I'd never get.

James described his best present—Nintendo—in one sentence, but he went on and *on* about the present he never got, a pony.

"Every year I'd ask Santa Claus for a pony, and my folks would say, 'Santa can't fit a pony in his sack,' and I bought it until I learned there wasn't no Santa Claus—"

"Just this year," Jason cracked.

"Shut up—and I asked my dad why I couldn't have a pony, and finally he said I just can't. That's it." He dropped his paper to his side. "I really wanted that pony, too."

I could picture a younger James, disappointed Christmas after Christmas. I'd never seen him in that light before.

Corky went next. The present he wanted but never got was a real timber wolf cub. His parents said it was too hot here for a wolf, and anyway it would probably ruin their white carpet.

"And he's rich," Teresa said to me. "You'd think he'd get anything he wants." The present she wanted but never got was her father to come back home. She hadn't seen him since she was two. The class was silently respectful as she returned to her seat.

As I heard about the presents they never received, I began to see a pattern. Most of the things they wanted would never fit in Santa's sack. Jason wanted to be on the Little League team, but he wasn't good enough. Ginger wanted her parents to get back together. Robert hoped to go to a camp that specialized in art, but his parents couldn't afford it. Bruce shyly admitted he once wanted a stuffed rabbit, but his parents thought he was too old for stuffed toys. He cheerfully took the razzing from the others when they promised to get him a teddy bear.

Our beauty queen, Rosemary, wanted, of all things, a chemistry set! "I guess my mom thought I'd blow up the house," she said with a laugh. But from her tone, I could tell she really wanted that chemistry set. Now she experimented with makeup.

When the lunch bell rang, no one jumped up and bolted for the door. We sat dazed, reluctant to break the spell.

"Let's go eat, shall we?" Mr. Schaffer invited. He walked out with Rosemary, who chatted with him all the way down the hall.

The rest of us ambled behind, talking about our papers and what we would do when *we* had kids. I wished more than ever I had a disappointing Christmas to contribute. Because the others had made revealing confessions, they seemed to be closer. Now they had something in common besides bad behavior.

"Hey, Austin," Corky teased. "Are you going to ask for socks again this Christmas?"

"You know why your parents never got you that wolf cub?" I fired back. "Because they already had one. You."

He laughed and I did, too.

Suddenly it didn't matter if I got an A on my paper. I wondered if I had answered the second part of the question honestly after all. *Was* my life so perfect up until the time I was exiled to the Spitball Class?

In a way, I was like the stiff little dancer in my jewelry box, twirling to the same tune. Doing the same things, hanging out with the same friends, year after year. Where did Austin Sommers go when the lid was closed? I asked myself.

Now that things were changing, maybe I would find out.

Chapter

7

✿ "I managed to get your library privileges reinstated," Mr. Schaffer announced one Monday morning. "Your privileges have been revoked since the beginning of the year, but I thought you deserved another chance. You won't let me down, will you?"

The kids exchanged excited glances.

Every Monday the sixth graders had library period. Our class was supposed to go in the morning, the same time as the T and G class. I couldn't decide if that ridiculous combination was a scheduling fluke or somebody's idea of a joke. The Spitball kids made the T and G kids seem smarter and more talented, while the T and G kids made the Spitball kids look as if their pictures ought to be hanging in the post office.

The Spitball Class had only been allowed in the library once the whole year. I wasn't there then, and

I was afraid to ask what had happened. Now we were going again.

Ignoring Mr. Schaffer's warning, our class entered the library like a herd of hyperactive buffalo shoving to be first at the watering hole.

"Mr. Schaffer's class, over by the windows," the librarian ordered, attempting to corral the troublemakers where they'd do the least damage. It was clear she didn't want us anywhere near the terrarium and other breakables.

I saw Patty and Erin sitting with Bailey Hoffman at one of the small tables near the media center. With a quick glance away I headed toward the windows with the rest of my class.

"Austin!" Erin stood and waved. "Over here!"

The library wasn't strict about seating arrangements—library period wasn't like a regular class. Since sixth graders were too old for story hour, the librarian let us work independently on reports or choose books for free reading. Except for the worst offenders (everybody but me in Room 24), we could roam and sit where we wished.

Now Patty joined Erin in beckoning me over to their table.

Maybe they want to apologize, I thought with a flutter of hope. Maybe they want to be friends again. I decided to give them a chance.

I walked over to the media center and pulled out the empty chair at their table. "Hi," I said.

"Hi," said Patty and Erin.

"Do you have any gum?" Bailey asked bluntly. She was wearing a denim miniskirt and a T-shirt with a picture of the world on it. Printed over the world was the slogan "Been There, Done That."

"I have some sugarless. Is that okay?" I fished the gum package from my shoulder bag and handed it to Erin, who was closest.

"Thanks." Erin took one stick, then passed my pack around the table. Patty took a single stick like Erin, but Bailey helped herself to three.

"That's all we wanted," she said, shoving the mostly empty pack across the table to me. I felt like a private being dismissed by a general.

"What do you mean, that's all you wanted?" Anger boiled up inside of me. "You mean you called me over here for *my* gum and now you want me to toddle off to my corner? Who was your slave last week?"

Erin tried to smooth things over. "She didn't mean it that way, did you, Bailey?" Bailey shrugged. "She only meant that you might be bored here with us. We're working on a paper together, about red giants and white dwarfs."

"Really? Then you've got the wrong books." I nudged a thick volume on astronomy. "Fairy tales are in the little kids section."

Bailey snickered. "For your information, red giants and white dwarfs are types of *stars.*" Her snooty tone indicated it was obvious I would never be allowed to

76

mop the T and G classroom floor, much less be transferred there. I wanted to stuff that big thick book up
her left nostril.

"Austin can sit here, if she wants," Patty said, moving her papers. "Come on, Austin."

"No, thanks. I'm going to sit with my class." I
wouldn't sit at the same table with Bailey Hoffman if
you paid me a million dollars.

"Don't be mad," Erin said, as if I was being totally
unreasonable. "You don't really want to sit with those
maniacs. Look at that guy. Can you believe him?"

James was balancing the globe on the end of his
index finger, like he was Magic Johnson. When the
globe bounced and hit the carpeted floor with a dull
thunk, Mr. Schaffer snatched it before James slam-
dunked it into the wastebasket.

"You can't expect much from boys," Bailey pro-
nounced. "It's those *girls* who blow me away. That
one"—she pointed to Rosemary—"has on at least a
pound of makeup. And the one with the streaked
hair—where does she get her clothes? The Salvation
Army would reject those pants."

Erin and Patty laughed.

After hearing Teresa's essay, I felt uneasy about
running down the Spitball kids. Maybe those pants
were all Teresa had to wear today. "You shouldn't
make fun of people," I said.

Erin snickered. "Austin, those aren't *people*.
They're the kids from Room Twenty-four."

Not people! When did Erin get so critical? She didn't know anything about those kids. Nobody did, really. I wanted to tell them what I had figured out about my class. They weren't so bad. They just started out life on the wrong foot.

I did that once, in a race. Back in second grade we were supposed to run the ten-yard dash. I lined up with the other kids, but when the race began, I was facing the wrong way! It took me a few seconds to get turned around and running in the right direction, but I never caught up with the others. The Spitball kids were like that—they just couldn't catch up with the regular kids.

Erin and Patty might have understood if Bailey Hoffman wasn't there. They believed everything Bailey said.

Erin underscored my point with her next remark. "It's a known fact those kids are losers. Rejects."

I lifted my chin. "I suppose you think I'm a loser and a reject, too?"

"Nobody said that," Patty rushed to respond. "It's just that— Well, you've changed since you got in that class."

I've changed! I didn't think I had, but maybe it was time I *did.*

"Maybe I have changed," I said levelly. "I finally found out who my *true* friends are. In the future I'd appreciate it if you'd stop badmouthing my class."

Even Know-It-All Bailey was stunned into silence.

I reached over and took back the two extra sticks of gum Bailey left on her notebook. "Didn't your mother teach you not to be greedy?" With that parting shot, I stalked away.

Over by the windows my class was talking too loud, disrupting the whole library. I could tell from the librarian's discussion with Mr. Schaffer that our library privileges were going to be taken away again, this time probably for good.

I tossed the sticks of gum and what was left of the pack on the table and said, "Chew this and be quiet a minute. I have to tell you guys something."

There was a brief scuffle for the gum, then Corky asked, "What is it? Did you finally get your transfer?"

"Awww. I hope you're not leaving." Ginger chomped the gum with mighty motion. "We'll have to go back to being three girls and five boys."

"I'm not leaving yet," I said. "It's about our class. Everybody in the school calls us terrible things, just because we're in Room Twenty-four."

Corky snorted. "This is news? I told you when you first came that the school dumps on us."

"We're the school joke," Robert added unnecessarily.

"But you don't have to be!" I said. "Everybody makes fun of you because you give them reason to."

"If I had my way, I'd punch those nerds out," said Teresa.

"You can't go around punching out everybody who says something nasty about the class," I told her.

79

"Yeah. You'd be smacking kids all day long," Bruce pointed out.

I frowned. This discussion was heading in the wrong direction. "I'm not talking about hitting. I'm talking about changing your image."

"How? Change the number over our door? Okay, we'll be Room Thirty-one from now on," Corky suggested with a grin. The others giggled. Thirty-one was the number of the Talented and Gifted class.

"For one thing, you've got to be serious," I insisted. "It's not that hard to be a regular class. Just act like the others. You're the ones who make yourselves outcasts."

Now Corky frowned. "We never had a choice to be a regular class. They took our choice away when they stuck us in Room Twenty-four."

I looked at the circle of faces around me. They weren't rejects. They were just kids who'd got bum raps. Even worse, they *believed* what everyone said about them—that they were awful, worthless, no-good.

I remembered something else about that second-grade race. I remembered how I wanted to hide when the others laughed because I ran the wrong way, but I turned around and ran anyway. Though I finished absolute dead last, nobody made fun of me because I did run the race.

This class had to run the race. Of course, I couldn't tell them that. Maybe reverse psychology would work.

"Well," I said, as if sweeping the whole idea from my mind. "If you think it's impossible to change, then I guess it is. If you're *afraid* to try—"

"Who's afraid?" James said. "Me and Jason aren't afraid of anything, are we, Jase?"

"I'm not scared of nothing, either," Teresa put in.

Corky was the only one who might see through my little scheme. "What do you care what people think of us, Austin? As soon as your transfer comes, you're out of here. You'll go back to your nicey-nice friends, and we'll still be the school rejects."

"My nicey-nice friends aren't that nice," I stated flatly. "They aren't even my friends anymore." Out of the corner of my eye, I saw Erin, Patty, and Bailey watching me, heads bent close. I knew they were whispering about me. "Listen," I said, with more conviction than I'd felt since I was assigned to the Spitball Class, "as long as I'm in this class, I don't want to be the school joke. Even if *you* do."

Before I could say more, library period was over. Corky and the others burst out of the room and down the hall.

Mr. Schaffer noticed me lagging behind the others. He shuffled along beside me, imitating my dejected gait.

"Some days are worse than others," he said, trying to kid me out of my gloomy mood.

I managed a weak smile. "I wish I could believe that."

"Well, you'll probably be transferred out soon, but the others . . ." He didn't have to finish his sentence. We both knew the Spitball kids would never be let out on good behavior.

"They don't *have* to be the worst class in the school," I said. "I told them, but they wouldn't listen."

"Now you know how *I* feel," he said, still teasing. Then he said seriously, "You can't make the kids in Room Twenty-four change. Neither can I. They have to *want* to change."

I sighed. The Spitball kids would never want to change. They liked being the worst class in the world. It gave them status. Being at the very bottom was important to them. They intended to keep their place as absolute, dead last.

It was a nice day for dunking the principal. Although it was mid-November, it wasn't really cold yet. The dunking stand had been set up on the blacktop, where everybody could get a good view. The entire school had been let out for the afternoon. Teachers and students were gathered in a ring around the stand.

We had been waiting all year for this moment. Last year, at the end-of-school assembly, Mr. Wren challenged the students of Freeman to read five thousand books over the summer. If we did, we could throw baseballs and dunk him. Even though I knew I was moving, I read books all summer, along with everyone else. I logged the titles of the books I read on a sheet the teachers handed out at the assembly. I read almost a hundred books, and Chester read seventy-two. Mom mailed our sheets to Freeman before we left for Florida.

I was glad I was back to see the principal fall in a tub of water!

Mr. Wren appeared, dressed in a baggy clown suit and a red rubber nose. The students cheered as he climbed into the harness that swung over the vat of cold water. The pitchers took aim, but Mr. Wren held up a hand. He had a few words to say first.

"When I issued the challenge at the end of last year, I knew you'd come through! You all want to see your principal soaking wet!" Everybody laughed. "But to be honest," Mr. Wren went on, "I never thought you'd read nearly *twice* as many books as I asked. The teachers of Freeman and I salute you for a job well done. I hope you continue reading books. Are the pitchers warmed up?"

A bunch of kids in the front answered with a loud, "Yeah!" They had been specially chosen to throw the baseballs, three from each grade, including kindergarten. Because there were five sixth-grade classes, two of the classes did not have a pitcher selected from their room. The sixth-grade teachers drew straws and pitchers were chosen from Room 31 and Room 29. It was no surprise that nobody was picked from Room 24. Mr. Schaffer wasn't there when the drawing took place, so we weren't sure that Room 24 was even in the hat.

Our class stood near the basketball court, a little away from the main group.

Mr. Wren began swinging in the harness. He stuck out his tongue, daring the first few kids to knock him into the water. The little kids threw wildly, laughing shrilly.

The next bunch of kids had better aim. A second grader threw a bull's-eye and sent Mr. Wren splashing into the water. The school went crazy! He climbed back into the harness, dripping water, his thin hair plastered to his scalp. Before he was in the seat, a third grader knocked him into the water again. He came up, spluttering and laughing.

"You're a better thrower than those kids," James said to his brother. Jason nodded.

The Spitball kids were strangely quiet. They watched the dunking with a certain wistfulness. We all felt kind of left out, standing on the sidelines. This was a new feeling for me, but I realized the Spitball kids experienced it all the time.

After the dunking was over, we went back to our rooms. The mood in our class was different. Instead of yelling and roughhousing, the kids sat quietly in their seats. Mr. Schaffer noticed the change, too.

"I'm sorry no one from our class got to throw a ball," he said. "It's the luck of the draw, I'm afraid."

"No, it isn't," Corky said. "They didn't pick us on purpose. We didn't read any books."

Mr. Schaffer perched on the edge of his desk. "If

that's true, then do you feel you didn't deserve to throw a ball because you didn't participate in the reading program?''

Nobody answered.

Mr. Schaffer was quiet, too, assessing the situation. Finally he said, "I think that in addition to the All About Me project, we'll work on an All About Us project. It's time this class learned to work together. It's time you became a real class."

For the first time since I'd joined Room 24, no one disagreed with the teacher.

Chapter
8

❀ During the next few weeks, we worked on our All About Me projects. Mr. Schaffer put questions on the board, and we wrote short papers, almost like journal entries. He also read to us from *The Diary of Anne Frank,* a book about a Jewish girl who went into hiding with her family during World War II. So we were aware of *real* problems, and he even sneaked in a little math and science.

Once we had to describe our rooms at home. My paper wasn't very good because my bedroom in our rented townhouse had zero personality. We didn't plan to stay there long, so I didn't hang up any of my posters or unpack my cat statues. When I finished reading my essay describing my plain white walls and dull brown carpet, Robert handed me a sheet of typing paper. It was a drawing, not of a monster, but of a little boy with a dog.

"It's for your room," he said simply. "I copied it out of a book." Why did I ever think he was so beige?

I was stunned by his present. "Thank you," I said. "I'll keep it forever. And when you're a famous artist, I'll have one of your first drawings."

We also worked on All About Us projects. Mr. Schaffer let us work in small groups on assignments. Instead of running wild during recess, we did archery or gymnastics. At lunchtime there was less milk-carton popping and more real conversation among our group as we got to know one another better.

Mr. Schaffer noticed we were changing. "The rest of Freeman should see how this class has turned itself around," he said one morning. "There's an assembly this afternoon. This time you won't get kicked out."

We glanced anxiously at one another. Behaving properly through an entire assembly was a pretty tall order, but we had to enter the race sometime, I figured.

Our class *did* behave through the assembly, with only a little talking and cutting up. When the program was over, we filed out of the auditorium in a neat line. Teachers goggled at our orderly procession. They couldn't believe we were the same kids who couldn't walk down the hall without causing chaos. I couldn't believe it, either. Was it possible the worst class in the world was actually changing?

A fourth-grade teacher stopped by Mr. Schaffer's

door when we had returned to our class. "Great job. We never thought you'd last a week, much less tame those kids. You deserve a medal."

"No, *they* deserve the medal," Mr. Schaffer corrected. "I helped them, but they did all the hard work. They're really a terrific bunch of kids."

The terrific bunch of kids, hanging out the door to overhear this conversation, punched one another happily.

"We did it!" Corky crowed.

"Yes, you did," Mr. Schaffer agreed heartily. "You should be very proud of yourselves. You proved you *can* be like other classes."

"Let's not stop there," Corky said. "Let's aim to be the *best* class in the school."

I thought this was going too far, but the other kids were all for it. They'd had a taste of success and craved more.

Their chance to move into the spotlight came the next day when Mr. Wren made the morning announcements.

"Our annual holiday can drive starts tomorrow," he said. "The local homeless shelters need contributions. Any type of canned food will be welcome. Remember, the class that donates the most cans will have their name added to the brass plaque by the main office. Get in the spirit of giving. We are counting on you to make this the most successful can drive in the history of Freeman Elementary."

I could almost see the light bulb flash over Corky's head. "Mr. Schaffer!" he cried. "What's the record we have to beat in the can drive? To make it the most successful?"

"I don't know," Mr. Schaffer replied. "There's a file in the office. I'll go down and check."

As soon as he was out the door, Corky sprang up. "Listen, guys. We can win this can drive!"

"How can we win?" Ginger wanted to know. "There are only nine of us. The other classes have lots more kids. Even if they bring in one can each, they'd beat us."

"We won't let numbers stop us," Corky said fervently. "We *have* to get our class on that plaque, no matter what."

Mr. Schaffer returned with the dismal figures. Two years ago Mrs. Shute's fifth grade brought in the most cans—one hundred and seventy-three. In fact, her classes were winners on the plaque three years running.

"Has our room ever been on the plaque?" Bruce asked.

"Are you kidding?" James jeered.

Corky was out of his seat with his clipboard. "How many cans can you bring tomorrow?" he asked Robert.

"I don't know." Robert shrugged. "I don't know what's in our cupboards."

"What about you two?" Corky asked Jason and James. "You ought to be good for at least ten cans."

James said to Jason, "Let's bring in that asparagus stuff Mom keeps buying that we hate."

Mr. Schaffer seemed to be assessing the situation. "I don't really approve of this can drive," he said.

"Why not?" Corky challenged. "It's for a good cause. What are you—a Thanksgiving Grinch?"

"I believe in the cause," Mr. Schaffer answered. "It's the competition that bothers me. Some of the other teachers have complained, too, but apparently it's a school tradition. I disapprove because some kids will be able to bring in more than others."

"We can bring in lots!" Corky said.

"I don't doubt it, but I still don't see how having your name on a plaque will improve your school standing. Since you're so determined I talked to Mr. Wren when I went down to check on the past winners. To make the competition more fair—to balance out the number of students we have—Mr. Wren and I have agreed to match your contributions, can for can. If you bring in one can, we will each bring in one, so one can will equal three."

The cheers nearly shattered the windows.

"All riiiight, Mr. S.!"

"In exchange"—Mr. Schaffer shouted to be heard over the whoops of joy—*"you* will start doing homework."

"Awwww!"

"You can't be a regular class unless you start doing regular work," Mr. Schaffer stated. "It's not enough to win a can drive. School is more than that. I'll keep my end of the bargain if you keep yours."

With a sigh Corky said, "Well, if it's the only way we can get on the plaque . . ."

"Do we have any canned goods we can spare for the can drive at school?" I asked Mom when I got home from school.

"The cupboard is bare," she quoted. "Chester beat you to it."

Sure enough, there was a pile of cans on the counter with a sign bearing Chester's name.

"That little worm! He rides the same bus I do! How did he get here before me?"

Mom smiled. "He called me during lunch and told me to set aside the cans, that's how. Don't worry. The cupboard isn't really bare. Chester only asked for the food *he* liked. He said he wouldn't give any homeless person okra or kidney beans."

"Can I take all these?" I stacked chicken soup and tomato sauce on the counter.

"Sure." Mom watched me stack the cans. "I never see Erin or Patty anymore. You guys used to be tighter than ticks. Has something happened?"

"No," I said lightly, pretending to dust the top of a can of soup. "I see them at school. They're busy with homework a lot." Then all at once, surprising even me, I blurted out, "Oh, Mom, everything is terrible. Nothing's the same since we came back. Erin and

Patty are different. They don't want to do any of the stuff we used to do. I don't understand it." I left out the fact that they had a new friend.

Mom gently pushed my bangs off my forehead. "People change," she said. "At your age the changes come quickly. Erin and Patty are growing up. You are, too, though you might not be aware of it."

"I don't see how your friends can change so much you're not friends anymore," I said.

"I know you were disappointed when you weren't put in their class," she said. "But I think it's good you're in a class with new people. You need to get along with all kinds."

That was certainly an accurate description of Room 24. I wondered whether my mother would have been so eager for me to learn to get along with those particular new people, if she knew exactly what "all kinds" included.

The next morning Corky was waiting for me at the door with his clipboard. He checked off cans as we brought them in. "Only two, Bruce? You can do better than that. Seven, Austin. Great. Now, if you can bring in that many tomorrow—"

"This is all we got," Teresa said, plunking a bag of cans on the floor. "Don't ask me for any more. My grandma says we'll be homeless ourselves if we keep giving food away."

"All right, Teresa," Corky said. "We'll see what we can work out."

"What did you bring?" I asked him.

He produced a whole case of beef broth, undoubtably pilfered from the butler's pantry or wherever rich people store their canned goods.

True to their word, Mr. Schaffer and Mr. Wren matched our contributions, can for can. "If this drive isn't over soon, I'll be in traction," Mr. Schaffer joked, massaging his back after bringing in a loaded grocery sack.

But Corky wasn't satisfied. "Mrs. Schute's room brings in bags and bags every day. We have to get more."

"I can't," Robert told him. "My mom found out I took our dinner yesterday, and she hit the ceiling."

"Our mom won't let us bring in any more, either," James put in. Jason nodded.

Corky was obsessed with the can drive. He was like Rumpelstiltskin in the fairy tale, always wanting more and more gold. One morning I walked in to find our pyramid of cans had grown considerably.

Corky came in, dragging a box filled with cans. What was he up to now?

"Where did you get those?" I asked. "Did you knock over a grocery store, or what?"

"Not quite," he said evasively, stacking cans of peaches neatly along the bottom of the pyramid.

"Did you get those honestly?"

"Austin, all's fair in love and can drives," he said. "You've seen those kids from Mrs. Schute's room. They bring in a ton and a half every day."

Maybe they did, but at least they didn't steal from little kids, like I caught James and Jason doing.

I was walking past the primary rooms to return a library book when I stumbled on the Cruikshanks' blackmail ring.

Jason and James had cornered a first-grade boy by the drinking fountain.

"Gimme those cans," James ordered the boy, who clutched two cans of string beans to his chest.

"No," he said, sticking his chin up defiantly.

"Give 'em to me or I'll tell your teacher you spit in the water fountain," James threatened.

The boy's chin wobbled as he surrendered his cans of beans.

I broke in, snatching the cans from James. I gave them back to the little boy, who scooted into his classroom.

"Have you lost your mind?" I yelled at James. "Stealing from first graders? You can't take cans from little kids! It's unethical."

James shrugged. "Who cares? Corky wants cans."

I should have guessed that Corky Wainwright not only went along with their bullying tactics, but probably suggested the idea in the first place.

Back in Room 24 I confronted Corky. "I thought this class had turned over a new leaf. I thought we were going to be the best class in the school." My fists were clenched, I was so angry.

"We'll go back to being good after the can drive is

over," he assured me, tallying a new shipment from Ginger.

"It doesn't work that way! Either you've changed or you haven't!"

His eyes locked with mine. "You keep saying 'you.' Aren't you part of this class, Austin?"

I looked away. "Don't change the subject."

"If you are, then you'll be quiet until the drive is over. Room Twenty-four has never won anything. We *will* win this can drive."

But we didn't, not even illegally.

Jason was caught robbing cans from a kindergartner who screamed loud enough to bring authorities from three counties. Jason got a month of detention, and Mr. Wren ordered a full-scale investigation. Under questioning, Corky admitted he had been coming to school early to swipe cans from Mrs. Shute's room. The day I found him dragging a box in, he was late sneaking back from Mrs. Shute's class.

Mr. Schaffer was disappointed. "I don't think contests like this one bring out the best in people, so I can't blame you entirely. Have you learned anything from this experience? Do you feel good about this?"

Rosemary put up her hand. "I was glad to help the homeless."

Mr. Schaffer smiled. "That's good, Rosemary. Did anyone else learn anything?"

"Yeah," Jason said. "Don't get caught!"

After everyone in the school found out that Room

24 had cheated to win the can drive, the stories about our class started up again.

I ran into Erin and Patty and Bailey in the cafeteria the day the story leaked out.

"Nobody's ever cheated on a can drive before," Erin said, somewhat in awe. "They broke the mold with those kids."

"Those kids are rotten to the core" was Bailey's pronouncement. "They'll never reform."

"You shouldn't waste your time with them," Patty told me.

Bailey said, "Rumor has it you and that Corky what's-his-name both stole from Mrs. Shute's class."

Barely keeping my temper under control, I told her, "Don't believe everything you hear."

I was mad at her, but I was also mad because our class really blew it. Deep down I was afraid Bailey might be right. The worst class in the world *couldn't* reform.

Chapter *9*

❋ The atmosphere in Room 24 was glum, to say the least.

Mr. Schaffer tried to lighten the gloom. "The can drive was a big success this year. You helped. You *did* bring in a lot of canned goods."

Which we didn't get credit for. Mrs. Shute's class retaliated by claiming Corky stole more cans than he actually had. They confiscated at least two bags that we brought in legitimately. "Cheaters seldom prosper," my father always said. Sometimes parents can be very annoying.

Friends—and I use the term loosely—were worse than annoying.

"Is your class still robbing little kids?" Erin taunted during the next library period. Her tone jabbed at me like a knife. Was this any way for the president of the sixth grade to talk? Obviously she'd been taking snooty lessons from Bailey Hoffman.

"They did it for a good cause," I defended lamely.

Patty came over to get a book for Bailey. "I don't know how you stand those criminals," she remarked, overhearing my conversation with Erin.

I watched her hand hesitate over taking down a book. She was afraid of choosing the wrong title for Miss High-and-Mighty. At the round table apparently reserved for Bailey Hoffman and her royal servants, Bailey twirled her pencil impatiently. Patty was taking too long. I was surprised Bailey actually did her own writing. Erin probably held the pencil for her.

"At least I'm not a slave," I said. "I don't have to wait on people hand and foot like you do."

"I'm not a slave," Patty said, contradicting her statement as she added a thousand-pound atlas to the towering stack of reference books. "I'm just doing Bailey a favor. Don't you do your friends favors anymore, Austin?"

"Yeah. The biggest favor I do is stay away from them."

That one zinged home. Patty, who was always more sensitive than Erin, looked hurt. She bit her lip, shifting the heavy books. "You never used to say things like that. You're not the same since you went to that class."

"As if I had a choice." I was tired of people assuming I had turned into Frankenstein just because I was in Room 24.

"And I *am* the same," I said stoutly. "I still like Monopoly and old black-and-white reruns on TV. I still like books that make me cry. Remember how we read *Little Women* over and over, especially the part where Beth died?" She nodded, remembering. "I'm still me. I'm just not a doormat now."

"You were never a doormat!"

I waved away the comparison. "A puppy dog, then. You know how puppies are—everybody in the whole world is their friend? I'm not that dumb anymore." I whirled around to go sit with my class.

"Austin—" Patty said behind me, but she didn't say it very loud.

I didn't answer her.

If a photographer had snapped our picture at lunch, he could have labeled the photograph *Dejection.* The very word hung over the Spitball table like the smell of old garbage. In fact, there *was* a smell of old garbage—our table was right next to the trash cans. But I'd never noticed it before that day.

Usually the activity level at our table was so feverish, I wouldn't have noticed a drowned skunk in my beef stew (at least, the menu *claimed* it was beef). But that day nobody cracked a joke, or zapped a straw wrapper, or threw peas.

Bruce popped his milk carton halfheartedly. Instead of a big satisfying *bang,* the carton sounded more like a fizzled firecracker.

I couldn't stand it another second.

"Listen, guys, it's not the end of the world. So we didn't win the can drive. So what? There'll be other drives."

"Not in this school," Robert said sourly. "Next year we'll all go to junior high."

The only way anyone from Room 24 would make it to junior high would be under an assumed identity, but I decided not to bring that up. They were all depressed enough.

"The year's not even half over," I said. "We can still win—something." I couldn't imagine what, though.

Corky leaned back in his chair. He hadn't touched his lunch, not that I could blame him. The mystery meat in our stew had a suspicious green tinge.

"Why the cheerleader act?" he asked. "What do you care if we win anything? All you're angling for is a transfer. As soon as it comes, you'll leave us in the dust."

"My transfer might not come through for a long time," I said. I had checked just that morning. Miss Hopkins informed me that a kid *was* moving, but he was in fourth grade. For an instant, I actually considered taking his place.

But Corky's remark made me think. Did I really care if Room 24 became a regular class? I was going to jump ship as soon as my transfer came in. Why do all that work and then leave? So I could say I was the person responsible for turning the worst class in the world into a normal class?

"It's all your fault," Ginger accused. Her voice rose to a squeaky pitch as she imitated me. " 'Get involved in school activities.' Well, we got involved and look what happened. Now we're the laughingstock of Freeman."

"We were already the laughingstock of Freeman before the can drive," Rosemary pointed out. "You shouldn't have set us up to think we could be anything but," she added to me.

"I never told you guys to steal from Mrs. Shute's room! Or rob the little kids! It was *your* idea to win the can drive. Get on the plaque, that's all you talked about. Why couldn't you just donate cans? Why did you have to try to be the best?"

Corky stared at me in disgust, as if any two-year-old could figure out the reason. "Because," he said witheringly, "we're tired of being the worst."

A little piece of Room 24's gloom broke off and followed me home.

I slammed the door to our house, completely forgetting Chester was right behind me.

"Hey!" he cried. "You smooshed my nose!" His nose was fine, but the bill of his Redskins cap was bent.

"Sorry." I straightened his cap.

Mom came bounding in from the kitchen. Lately she'd been out every day with a real estate lady, looking at houses.

"Hi, guys!" she trilled. "How was school?"

"Great," Chester said.

"No comment," I said.

Mom let my remark pass. She was bursting to tell us her news. "Guess what? I found us the perfect house with a huge yard. Best of all, it's just a couple of blocks from our old house. You can both stay in Freeman."

My heart fell to my toes. A few months ago I would have rejoiced at the news. I was moving even closer to where Erin and Patty lived—and Bailey Hoffman.

"Austin," Mom prompted. "Aren't you glad? I thought you'd be turning cartwheels."

"Yeah, I'm glad," I said, though I didn't sound it. "But—maybe you should have looked more, Mom. You shouldn't have bought the first house you saw."

"I scarcely leapt at the first structure with four standing walls. I've been pounding the pavement with real estate agents since we came back to Virginia last October." She tugged my hair. "Of course, the house isn't on our old street."

"It isn't?"

"No, it's a couple blocks over, in the newer section."

"Not on our old street?" That was a little better. Maybe I could live with it, as long as I didn't have to pass Bailey Hoffman every day of my life.

Mom promised we'd all go see the new house when Dad got home from work. She went in to start supper.

Chester switched on the TV. Flopping in front of the set, he began coloring a map of the United States for homework.

I didn't feel like watching TV or doing homework. My thoughts were as jumbled as the crayons in my brother's art box. "I wish we'd never moved," I said. "It's like we were in Florida six years instead of a few weeks. Nothing's the same since we came back."

"Who wants things to stay the same?" Chester bit the paper off a crayon with his teeth.

"Don't do that. The crayon may make you sick."

Naturally he didn't listen. "I liked Florida. It was fun, like a real long vacation. Now I have friends in two states." Chester wrote to a few kids in his old Florida third grade. He was young enough to view each move as an adventure, instead of a disaster. He collected friends along the way.

"I don't have friends in any state," I said morosely, fiddling with the worn-out laces on my sneakers.

If we hadn't moved, Bailey Hoffman would be living in another house—maybe even this very townhouse, though I couldn't see her putting up with plain white walls for a second—and I'd still be best friends with Erin and Patty.

Or would I? Was my friendship with them fraying at the edges, like the laces on my sneakers?

"You never want to be friends with anybody but Erin and Patty," Chester said with remarkable insight for an eight-year-old. "You didn't like anybody in Florida. Now you don't like anybody in your class."

103

"You aren't in Room Twenty-four," I said.

"I like your class."

"You do? *Why?*" I knew he shouldn't have bitten those crayons.

Chester picked up a yellow one and began coloring in Kentucky. "Because it's neat. It's not like the other classes."

"That's certainly true."

"You'll have fun on Sports Day," Chester went on, outlining the Mississippi River.

Sports Day! I forgot about the annual Freeman Sports Day in April. All the classes competed against one another in different games, like a mini-Olympics. Last year Erin, Patty, and I helped our class come in first. It was a lot of fun. I shivered at the thought of participating in an All-School Sports Day with Room 24.

"You'll probably win for your class again this year," said Chester.

"I doubt it. That class never wins anything."

"How come? They're fast runners. I see them at recess."

"You see them running *away,* usually from people they've just hit or tripped," I said wryly. "Not quite the same as running *toward* a finish line in a race."

"They'll win if you're there," Chester said staunchly. "You can run real fast, Austin."

I *was* a good runner. After that disastrous dash in second grade, I had worked on becoming a good runner. The boys in Room 24 were fast when they put their crafty little minds to it. Maybe we *could* win if we pulled together. Where had I heard that before? Then I remembered the speech Mr. Schaffer gave me when we both first went to Room 24. He had also said the others in the class looked up to me. I didn't believe it at the time, but I was beginning to think it might be true.

I went into my room. It was awfully dull, with those bare white walls, but we would be moving again soon. The only nice thing I had unpacked was my grandmother's jewelry box. I opened the lid. The ballerina twirled to the tinkling music. The familiar tune was comforting.

I studied the drawing Robert had made me. It was nice having something different on my wall besides my same old posters. Robert's picture reminded me of my class. Corky had accused me of never being one of them, and maybe he was right.

I only pretended to be one of them, but I never put my heart into being a member of the class. I held back from belonging to Room 24, always hoping for a better deal to come along.

Well, I asked myself. Was I one of them or not? If Room 24 was ever going to gain respect, they needed me. But that wasn't all—I needed them. I needed to make friends with somebody besides Erin and Patty.

I closed the lid of my jewelry box. It was time to change the tune, try new dance steps.

*   *   *

I plunked a sheaf of pink announcement sheets on Corky's desk. "The All-School Sports Day is in five weeks," I proclaimed. "We can win at least half of those events. We might even snag the trophy."

He stared at the announcement, then at me. "You must be kidding."

"No, I'm not." By now the others were listening with out-and-out disbelief. I knew this wouldn't be easy.

"What makes you think we want to do this?" Corky asked.

"Because it's our chance to win something legally. You can't cheat or rob during a relay race. And we're all good in sports." I wasn't too sure about that. In the old days, before Mr. Schaffer got us organized, the class spent recess disrupting games or hogging the swings so the little kids couldn't use them. Still, I figured they had some natural talent, well hidden.

"We could be a real part of Freeman," I said enticingly. "We'd have the Sports Day trophy for this year."

"You're saying 'we,' " Corky said. "Does this mean you're in with us?"

I took a deep breath. "Yes."

"Well, you'll need a coach," came a voice from the doorway.

Mr. Schaffer set a box on his desk. He pulled out a green T-shirt with white letters across the front that read "I'm in Room 24 and Proud of It."

"What do you think?" he said. "There's one for each of you."

The T-shirts were perfect, although the motto "I'm in Room 24—Want to Make Something of It?" would have been more fitting.

"How did you know we were going to try for the trophy?" I asked him.

"A wild guess. I knew this class would get tired of being on the bottom. Now you're finally ready to pull together. You have no place to go but up."

Rosemary applied green eyeshadow to match her new T-shirt. "We sure can't get any lower," she said.

Chapter 10

❋ The green T-shirts were the only coordinated thing about our sports team.

Mr. Schaffer arranged for us to have the playing field to ourselves after school every day. After two minutes on the field the first day, I realized with a sinking heart I had exaggerated the athletic talents of Room 24—by about five hundred percent.

"All right, people," Mr. Schaffer said, relishing his new role as track coach. "Let's see your form. Run a lap around the field."

"The whole way?" James grimaced.

We straggled. Even the speediest runners loped along like anteaters. The rest weren't that fast. As I crossed the finish line first—which I could have done with both eyes shut hopping on one foot—it occurred to me that not only did this class lack form, we wouldn't be track stars in twenty years, much less a few weeks.

"Not bad," Mr. Schaffer fibbed, not meeting our eyes. "Okay, double line, facing one another. Let's do some throwing and catching."

He tossed a ball to me, low. Bending my knees, I caught it, then threw the ball to Corky. Corky threw the ball to Rosemary, who was standing opposite him. She missed. Even worse, she didn't even *know* she had missed.

Mr. Schaffer retrieved the ball and tossed it neatly to Bruce. Bruce was busy scratching at the time. He missed, too. Teresa hurled the ball like a guided missile, knocking the wind out of Robert.

"Ooooh! She killed me!" He rolled around, clutching his stomach.

Teresa didn't waste any sympathy on him. "Quit bellyaching. Honestly," she complained to Ginger. "Boys are such wimps."

"We are not," Robert huffed, getting up.

"Maybe if we had water balloons—" Jason suggested.

"Heaven forbid." Mr. Schaffer pretended to wipe sweat from his forehead. "See that red ribbon? I've tied one end of it to the basketball pole. Follow the ribbon wherever I put it. If the ribbon goes over something, you go over it too. Climb if you have to. No going around."

He blew the whistle. We formed a ragged line with James in the lead. I positioned myself at the end because it seemed the safest place to be.

Two blasts from the whistle and we were off, jogging

across the blacktop, following the ribbon trail down the hill to the playground equipment. The ribbon led us around the seesaws and between the swings. We had to dodge jangling chains to get through. Then I saw the ribbon was threaded through the rungs of the monkey bars.

James was pretty good, but Corky sprang up and hauled himself across the bars. He zipped down on the other side and crawled through the jungle gym, following the red tape. Corky was our brightest hope.

The others were another story. Bruce couldn't pull himself hand over hand across the monkey bars, so he dropped to the ground to walk to the next part of the course.

"No cheating!" Mr. Schaffer yelled, blowing the whistle.

"I can't do it!" Bruce whined.

"Yes, you can! Try again."

He still couldn't manage the bars, so Robert put Bruce on his shoulders and Bruce lightly touched each bar. Then poor Robert had to go back and walk the bars himself. The girls were worse, but Mr. Schaffer wasn't as hard on them. I pulled myself across, my palms stinging from the rungs.

Meanwhile Bruce was stuck in the next stage of the course, the jungle gym.

"Lose a few pounds, will you?" Robert muttered, pushing Bruce through to the other side.

Rosemary walked the course as if she were strolling

through the park. What she didn't feel like climbing or crawling through, she ambled around.

"Mr. Schaffer, Rosemary's cheating," Ginger bellowed. "Make her crawl on the ground like the rest of us."

"Do I have to?" Rosemary appealed to the teacher. "I don't want to get dirty." She wasn't exactly dressed for track practice. She had on tight, below-the-knee pants, a little ballet skirt, and an off-the-shoulder top with a leotard underneath. The sleeves of another shirt were tied jauntily around her waist. She looked like a tennis-playing ballet dancer.

The last segment of the obstacle course was tricky. The ribbon led us over the wooden climber and spiraled down the rope at the end. We were supposed to swing over a puddle.

"Hey, cool!" James cried. "Just like in the marines." He gave a rebel yell as he grabbed the rope and swung over the puddle. Corky also swung over successfully.

Bruce, of course, fell in. Robert, who was behind him, was so busy concentrating that he didn't see Bruce in the puddle and fell in on top of him.

Jason couldn't resist joining the party. Soon half the class was rolling around in the mud.

The whistle shrilled. "Get out of that puddle!" Mr. Schaffer barked. Four kids struggled out of the mud, giggling. Mr. Schaffer looked at them sternly. "Clearly, practice is over for today. Tomorrow, be prepared to work. The only way you will win any event on Sports Day is by pulling together as a team. There will be no individual heroes on that day."

Not that our class could supply any.

The next day we brought our shirts to class.

"Put them on," Mr. Schaffer said. "Over your regular clothes. You're going to wear them all day, not just during practice. I want you to get used to being a team."

Then he asked us to turn our desks over. I wasn't sure I heard him right. He nodded. "That's right, Austin."

We flipped our desks over so the legs were sticking up in the air, just like they were that day when Mr. Schaffer and I first walked into Room 24.

"Now line up by the blackboard. Jason, you're first. I want you to run around the classroom and jump over each desk."

Jason goggled at him. Had the teacher finally cracked?

"Go on," Mr. Schaffer urged. "Imagine a new teacher is arriving today. You want to impress him, Room Twenty-four-style."

Jason sprinted around the room, hurdling the desks like an Olympic star. He didn't trip over a single one. James flew behind his brother, jumping even higher. We ran and jumped like training ponies. Sometimes we bumped into one another. We'd just laugh and go on.

"Great!" Mr. Schaffer said. "You seem to jump better indoors that outside." He put his wastepaper basket in the middle of the room. It was filled with wadded-up paper. Dumping the basket on the floor, he said, "Each of you take five or six paper wads. Then I want you to form two teams, facing one another. The object of this game is to throw the paper at the person opposite you and at the same time catch the wad he'll throw to you. Keep the paper flying. You're experts at that."

Loaded with ammunition and enthusiasm, we lined up against two sides of the room. At the teacher's signal we began throwing.

I pitched a paper wad to Ginger. Tossing and catching in a split second was hard but fun. I got bonked on the head so many times, I couldn't stop laughing. Once Ginger threw her paper wad too high. It bounced off the light fixture, then ricocheted off Mr. Schaffer's nose, which made us laugh even more.

Soon we were all in stitches, but more paper wads stayed in the air than landed on the floor. I caught the rhythm of Teresa next to me. By the end of the drill, we were all tossing and catching in unison.

"Well done," Mr. Schaffer praised. "You deserve a reward."

Going over to the supply cabinet, he pulled out a cooler he must have brought in before school. He pitched us each a juice box. As we sat comfortably on the floor, he passed around a bag of white-chocolate macadamia-nut cookies.

"Who knows the meaning of sportsmanship?" he asked.

Teresa raised her hand. "Sportsmanship is when you don't punch the guy out when he beats you. You just hit him a little bit."

Mr. Schaffer tried not to smile. "Close. Austin? Do you know the definition?"

"It's how you behave," I replied. "It's playing fair and being a good loser. You don't pout if you lose."

"It's also being a good winner, wouldn't you say?" he said. "A good winner doesn't brag or lord it over the losers. In our case, sportsmanship is playing as a team. Remember there are no individual winners on Sports Day. Only winning *teams.*"

He never let us forget that, whether we were practicing out on the field after school or practicing in the classroom. Once we started working together as a team, our regular lessons became more interesting. We began pulling for each other, cheering each other's victories. We were all glad when Jason got a C on a spelling test and when Rosemary solved a math problem on the board without any help.

I began hearing new music in my head. I was no longer Austin of the Erin-Patty-Austin crowd, but Austin Sommers, myself.

At the end of each day we stood in front of the room and said something new about ourselves, to help us overcome performing in public.

During those end-of-the-day sessions, I learned that

Corky wished his parents didn't have such important jobs, so they'd be home more. Ginger said she'd gladly change places with him. She wished her mother would get off her case.

Rosemary admitted her real name was not Rosemary at all, but Dorothy! As soon as she could talk, she ditched her name and became Rosemary, which suited her better.

I told the class about the wildlife in Florida—the skittering lizards and cockroaches big enough to saddle and ride. Everybody laughed. I never realized I could tell funny stories. With my old friends, I wasn't considered the funny one. Then I mentioned the new house on Graycliff Avenue we would be moving into in a few weeks.

"I live on Graycliff!" Ginger said. "We'll be neighbors."

"I live on Mapleview," Rosemary added eagerly. "We can ride the same bus to school."

I wasn't sure how I felt about having Room 24 kids as neighbors, but at least I wouldn't be on Bailey's bus anymore.

James made an astonishing confession when it was his turn. Fidgeting in front of the blackboard, he cleared his throat, then said, "I just want you guys to know I really didn't want to get left back, but since I did, I'm glad I'm with you." His face was beet red, and he sat down abruptly.

Mr. Schaffer covered the awkward silence. "You

know, James, you can catch up to your grade level if you try. It means working extra-hard in here and going to summer school."

"School all year round?" James was doubtful.

"Well, think about it."

Teresa raised her hand, something she would never have done two months ago. "I don't hate school as much as I used to."

Mr. Schaffer looked ecstatic. "Really? How wonderful."

"Don't go overboard. I still hate school," she added. "But not as much. I like it a teeny bit more every day, though."

Ginger asked permission to leave her seat. She walked up to Mr. Schaffer's desk and plunked down two quarters. "I'm giving this back to you," she said.

Mr. Schaffer pocketed the money. "You pay your loans back promptly. You'll be a shrewd business-woman someday."

Ginger was grinning as she returned to her seat. She had ripped off the teacher the first day, making him pay ransom for his briefcase and roll book, but Mr. Schaffer had treated the incident as if it were a loan. He had a way of making us all feel good about ourselves.

Now Corky raised his hand.

"Yes, Corcoran?"

"I just want to say you're okay, Mr. S. You never gave up on us. Everybody else did." He paused. "By the way, you can call me Corky."

Mr. Schaffer acted as if he'd just received a wonderful present. "I didn't give up on you because I believe in you," he said. "None of you are dummies. With a little work, you can all be at grade level. In fact, I believe you'll zoom ahead. Look at the progress you've made already. You're doing great."

The class buzzed excitedly as we walked out to the playing field. Mr. Schaffer had convinced us we could do anything.

Sports Day was only a week away. Several classes practiced on the field, so we no longer had it to ourselves.

"There go the brains," said Robert. The Talented and Gifted class marched across the blacktop, knees high, chins up, as if they knew they were the best.

"They won't be any competition," Jason scoffed. "All the brains they got is between their ears!"

Everyone broke up at this remark. I laughed, too, but I knew Erin and Patty were both excellent runners. Bailey Hoffman could probably whip out gold medals in every sport including rugby and table tennis.

As if reading my mind, Bailey broke ranks to execute a perfect cartwheel. Then she moved into a handstand, her legs straight as a ruler. She walked on her hands beside her marching class. When her class halted, she jackknifed neatly to her feet, dusting off her palms.

She saw me and came over. Erin and Patty followed.

"What'd you think of that?" she asked, bold as brass.

I wasn't going to let her see I was impressed. "What, no high-wire act?"

Patty giggled.

Bailey was not amused. She sneered at the kids in my class, who were messing around on the playground equipment. "Your class is going to need a lot more than matching T-shirts. I hope those kids aren't going to be on the field next Friday. They'll ruin the chance for *serious* athletes to get better scores. Last year I ran the six-hundred in less than two minutes."

"Was your leg broken?" I asked insultingly. "We'll be in every single event next Friday, don't worry." But I *was* worried. Mr. Schaffer had filled us with confidence. I knew we still had a long way to go. What would happen when we lost? I could picture short-tempered Teresa hitting the guy who beat her "only a little bit."

The T and G teacher blew her whistle. "We have to go," Erin said to me. "Good luck next Friday."

I gave them our old thumbs-up sign. "Good luck to you guys!"

"We won't need it," Bailey said. "But *your* class will."

She was probably right, but I couldn't let her get away with her remarks. I had to unsettle her everlasting smugness.

"Hey, Bailey!" I yelled after her. "Have you seen that mouse yet?"

She stopped. "What mouse?"

"In my old room. You haven't seen him yet? He's cute."

"A *mouse*. In *my* room?"

"I guess you haven't seen him because he only comes out at *night*. The thing is, he likes to chew long hair." I flipped my short hair. "That's why I cut mine."

Her mouth gaped with horror. "A *mouse!* A hair-nibbling mouse lives in *my* room?"

I smiled innocently. "It's okay. He's real friendly." Then I stared at her left ear. "Hey, your hair looks shorter on that side."

"I don't believe you," she said, but her voice had an edge to it. She turned uncertainly to join her class.

I noticed with delight she kept tugging her hair over her left ear, trying to see if she had any mouse-nibbled split ends.

Chapter 11

❋ Freeman's All-School Sports Day was a huge event. We rolled off the buses, reported to our classes to take attendance, then the entire school streamed down to the playing field.

The field was decorated for the big day. Cloth-draped tables had been set up at the four corners as refreshment stations. Room mothers handed out cups of Gatorade or fruit pops to hordes of thirsty athletes. On a crepe paper-draped platform the trophy glinted in the sun, waiting for a new class to claim it.

I followed my class down the hill to the area where the older kids were milling around. To make things fair, Mr. Wren divided the school into three groups: first and second grades, third and fourth, and fifth and sixth. The kindergartners were too young to participate. Our opponents were our age or close to our age.

That way a little kid wouldn't get mowed down by a big sixth grader in a relay race.

I saw Chester in his grade group and waved. He waved back. Mom was supposed to come by later and help serve the picnic lunch. "I'll need a break from packing," she informed us at breakfast. We were moving into our new house the next weekend. Dad was invited to Sports Day, too, but he had to work.

I jogged in place to warm up. It felt neat to be outside the whole day. The sun was shining and the sky was clear. In the woods bordering the field, dogwood trees blazed scarlet.

Then I saw my ex-best friends with the T and G class. Erin and Patty and Bailey all had on matching navy shorts. Bailey wore her snooty "Been There, Done That" T-shirt. Her long hair was pulled up in a whale spout on top of her head. She looked confident and unruffled, but I knew now that she wasn't as cool as she appeared.

Mr. Schaffer called the members of Room 24 into a huddle. "I just received our morning schedule," he told us. "Because our class is smaller than the other sixth grades, we'll run against the odd fifth grade class for the dashes and relay races."

"We can beat those kids with one hand tied behind our back," James boasted.

"They may be younger, but you can bet Mrs. Shute will pit her best runners against us."

Not Mrs. Shute's class, I thought darkly, the first

doubt of the day deflating my buoyant mood. They already had it in for us because of the can drive fiasco.

While we performed warm-up stretches, Mr. Wren screeched into his portable microphone that several events would be going on at once in different parts of the playground.

Our group was doing the ten-yard dash at the far end of the field. Two fifth grade classes went first, then it was our turn to run against Mrs. Shute's fifth grade. Nine of her best runners were paired off with each kid from our class.

Ten-yard dashes went very fast. Kids on the sidelines yelled for their team, as pair after pair sprinted the short distance. My turn was over before I knew it. I crossed the line ahead of my opponent with ease.

Mr. Schaffer announced the winner. "Room Twenty-four!" he cried, unable to keep the pride out of his voice.

Teresa slapped my palms while Corky and Bruce and Jason leapt up in a high-five.

The fifty-yard dash was next. I sat down in the grass with Ginger to wait our turn.

"I've been watching that Bailey girl," she remarked, gazing across the field where the sixth graders pelted down their fifty-yard race course. "She's pretty good. So are her friends."

"I know Erin and Patty are good," I said. "We were on the same team last year."

She chewed a piece of grass thoughtfully. "Do you miss being on their team this year?"

Leaning back on my elbows, I did a donkey kick to keep my leg muscles flexed. "Well, we were really good in the relay races because we knew one another's times."

I deliberately evaded answering her question. The T and G class, small like ours, seemed to be winning every race without having to be matched up with younger opponents. I remembered how neat it was to be on the winning team last year. Then I remembered Mr. Schaffer's lectures on sportsmanship.

Mr. Howitz's fifth grade won the fifty-yard dash. Our class was good at short sprints but still had trouble going the distance. There were lots of glum faces in our group until Mr. Schaffer reminded us the day had only just begun.

"It's not over till it's over," he said.

Next we did the long jump. I have never been a good jumper and didn't care for this event. We had three tries each. My score wasn't great—barely five feet. I kept losing my balance and falling back, which cost me inches. Corky earned the highest score in our class—a magnificent five feet, eleven inches. My hopes ballooned again. We wouldn't know until the end of the day which class had won the long jump, since the other fifth and sixth grades were doing relay races.

When they finished racing, it was our turn. This was my best event, and I felt confident, especially after I saw the fifth graders Mrs. Shute picked from her class to run against us.

We would run in double heats on parallel tracks. Mr. Schaffer divided us into teams of five, letting Corky run twice, and gave me the baton. I was the lead runner in the first heat. Curling my fingers around the baton, I crouched in position.

"Don't just hand the baton to your teammate," he instructed. *"Slap* it into his palm." He gave the signal. "Ready? Set—Go!"

At the drop of his arm I shoved off from my left heel and flew around the circular track. Ginger was waiting for me. I slapped the baton into her hand, and she took off. Then I jogged into the sidelines and cheered for her. Ginger was a good runner, but she didn't slap Rosemary's palm with the baton. Rosemary fumbled the baton, never quite dropping it but not clutching it firmly, either. She lost us precious seconds that neither Robert nor Corky could regain.

On the second heat Corky was first and made up the time. He ran as if all the principals in the world were after him. Jason and then James followed, both running like cheetahs. Teresa almost let the baton fall, but she caught it and ran. Bruce was the last runner in the relay race.

I bit my thumbnail. Why had Mr. Schaffer put Bruce at the very end? Granted, it would have been suicide to put our worst runner in the lead, but if Bruce had been in the middle, a better runner could make up the time he was sure to lose.

"He's going to drop it," I moaned.

Teresa smacked the baton into his hand so hard, I could hear it crack. Bruce's hand must have hurt like anything, but it didn't slow him down. He ran faster than the wind! We screamed our lungs out for him.

He whizzed around the track, his short fat legs pumping. The fifth graders still had to pass the baton to the last runner. Bruce saw us and grinned. We had this one in the bag! Bruce raised his arm with the baton, a gesture of triumph—and took his eyes off the course.

He ran diagonally by our finish line into the fifth grade's track. He didn't officially cross the line! Before Bruce could get his bearings, the fifth grade's final runner grabbed the baton and sailed around the course, taking advantage of Bruce's mistake. They beat us by eleven whole seconds.

James pummeled Bruce with his cap. "You idiot!"

Mr. Schaffer stepped between them. "Stop it! What Bruce did could happen to anybody."

"I ran the wrong way one time," I said, hoping to lighten the mood. Bruce smiled gratefully. I knew he really wanted our class to win, but some things were impossible.

After the other fifth grades ran the relay race, it was time for lunch.

Mom was at a big table set up at the end of the blacktop, doling out plastic-wrapped sandwiches. "I saw you run."

I took a sandwich and an apple from a bowl. "Well, at least we won the ten-yard dash."

Chester came bobbing up. "Mom, guess what! I did the most chin-ups. I did fourteen!"

"Fourteen chin-ups," Mom said. "That's terrific. We'll have two champs in the family by the end of the day. Dad said he's taking us all out for pizza tonight."

"Yippee!" Chester skipped off to join his class.

I took my lunch over to the shade tree where a tight clump of green T-shirts were camped out. "Get to know your fellow students," Mr. Wren encouraged us before we broke for lunch. "That's the real purpose of Sports Day, to have fun."

We knew better. The real purpose of Sports Day was to win the All-School trophy.

Bailey Hoffman sidled up to me. I noticed Patty and Erin carrying cold drinks and sandwiches, Bailey's faithful slaves.

"I asked my father about that mouse," she said snippily. "And he said there weren't any mice in our house. He hired a pest control man to treat the house before we moved in, so there wouldn't be any fleas or cockroaches. Daddy said mice are pests, and they would have been killed, too."

"Mice aren't the only pests," I retorted, wondering what Mom would say if I told her the Hoffmans thought our house had bugs.

"Your class is up against ours this afternoon."

I gave her a fake smile. "May the best class win!" Parroting Mr. Schaffer's lectures in good sportsmanship, I was nice to the opposition, even though I hated her guts.

126

"We will." She spun smartly on one heel and strode over to the tree where Patty and Erin waited with her lunch.

Mr. Schaffer gave us a pep talk before the events resumed. "Remember, we are a *team*. Most of the games require cooperation. It takes all of us pulling together to win."

This time we were competing with sixth graders. We had another relay race, which we won. Then there was an obstacle course, which we lost.

We lost the shuttle run, too, but I think it was because we were paired up with the Talented and Gifted class for the first time all day. Both classes stood in a row behind a chalk line, facing another chalk line with two balls on it about thirty feet away. At Mr. Schaffer's signal, we were supposed to run to the other line, pick up a ball, bring the ball back to our starting line, go back, pick up the second ball and sprint across the starting line. Along the starting line, Room 24 kids alternated with T and G kids. Bailey Hoffman was opposite me.

Mr. Schaffer shouted "Go!" and everybody ran to get the first ball. It was like the first relay race, only worse. Our class kept dropping the ball.

"Butterfingers," Bailey taunted as she ran past me. Some sportsmanship!

We weren't busy every second of the day. A lot of the time we had to wait until the other classes in our group finished. I sat on the ground with the girls. Rosemary was showing us how to make a new kind of friendship bracelet with colored embroidery floss she brought in her pocket. I began braiding the intricate pattern in purple and gold.

"I think they're winning," Ginger said, nodding toward the Talented and Gifted class.

"No, they aren't," Teresa said. "They just *act* like they're winning. That's the way they act all the time."

I stopped weaving my bracelet. Teresa was right. The T and G class *acted* like winners, and they usually were.

The next event was the two-ball toss-and-catch. Our class was really good at this from our daily paper-wad drills. Again, the two classes formed two alternating lines, only this time we tossed the ball to a person from our class. Bailey was next to me, undoubtably to make me nervous. I wasn't going to let her rattle me this time.

On the count of three, we tossed the balls to each other. Whenever anyone missed a catch, that pair was eliminated. I quickly fell into Jason's rhythm, tossing and catching smoothly.

Beside me, Bailey kept up a steady stream of nasty remarks. "Look at the nerds. Couldn't catch that ball in a bucket."

"Shut up!" I hissed, and she turned to me, surprised. Sweet little Austin Sommers never told anyone to shut up.

In that split second she missed her partner's catch,

and they were eliminated. Bailey stomped off, hoping to make me miss, too, but I didn't. I concentrated on catching Jason's throws and pitching the ball back to him nice and easy. We were still throwing and catching when the last T and G pair struck out.

"Way to go!" Corky congratulated us.

I gulped a cup of Gatorade. Sports Day was nearly over. The teachers conferred during a break.

Mr. Schaffer reported the results of their deliberation. "Corky's long jump was the highest in any group," he announced proudly. "Plus our class was awarded extra points because each of you had to participate in every event. The bigger classes could let their kids take turns. We are tied for first place for the trophy."

"With who?" Robert asked.

Mr. Schaffer pointed to the Talented and Gifted class. "They're setting up a tie-breaker right now. Tug of war."

"Tug of war!" Corky's eyes gleamed.

It *was* war. The T and G kids were definitely our arch-rivals. They'd needled us all day, making snide remarks.

We formed our team carefully. The strongest boys, with Corky first, were placed at the front, then the girls were ranked according to strength. I was next to last, after Rosemary, who was our weakest puller. Bruce was last on the rope. Corky said it was important to have extra weight on the end.

The Talented and Gifted class chose their nine pullers with as much care. Shawn Zuskin led their team. Erin, Patty, and Bailey were included with the girls. I was delighted to see Bailey Hoffman take the middle position on the rope. I really, really wanted to drag that girl through the mud.

The mud puddle Mr. Schaffer had made for our obstacle course was still there, with more water added to make it super-gooshy. The entire school ringed the two teams. The playground roared with their yelling. Most of the kids cheered for the T and G class, but we didn't care. As I took my place behind Rosemary, I sensed a surge of newfound strength along the rope like a current of electricity. We were *ready*.

Mr. Wren's whistle blasted. I dug my heels in and yanked with all my might. Behind me, Bruce pulled so hard I was nearly leaning over backward. The rope burned my hand, but I wouldn't let go, even if it sliced my fingers off.

"We-are-unbeatable," Shawn grunted from the T and G team.

"You-don't-know-everything!" Teresa yelled back.

Gradually I felt the other side give. We were dragging them toward the puddle!

"Come *on!*" Corky cried hoarsely. "Fall in!"

"No way!" a T and G boy replied.

Suddenly there was a tug in the opposite direction, as if the T and G kids had got a second wind. Now *we* were being pulled toward the puddle!

Our team teetered on the brink of the puddle. I sensed everyone's concentration was shattered. We were no longer pulling together. We needed to be a team again.

"Spitballs!" I yelled in desperation, recalling the snowstorm that hit me and Mr. Schaffer our first day in Room 24. "Pretend it's a spitball blizzard!"

The strategy worked. The word *spitballs* was music to my classmates' ears. We all began pulling together again, with the force of a Class A spitball blizzard. We tugged and strained until the other team toppled into the puddle!

The greatest moment of my life came when I saw Bailey Hoffman land in squishy mud. Her famous "Been There, Done That" shirt was filthy!

"We won!" Teresa cried, dancing with me. "We won! The trophy will have our classroom number on it this year!"

"Now everybody will know the kids from Room Twenty-four aren't a bunch of losers," Corky crowed.

I felt so good I wanted to cry. Nothing I had ever won meant as much. Mr. Schaffer was already leading us up to the winners' platform.

In all the confusion Miss Hopkins called to me, "Austin! It's wonderful!"

"Thank you," I said. Even the secretary was proud of us.

"Oh, I didn't mean winning the trophy, dear. Though that's nice, too." She beamed at me. "You'll never guess—a boy from Miss Hunt's class is moving to Connecticut. You're finally going to get your transfer!"

I froze, stunned by the news. My transfer was the last thing I expected to hear!

My classmates stared at me, their jubilant expressions fading away. They looked as sad as the day they described their disappointing Christmases.

"Nice going, Austin," Corky said haltingly. "You finally got what you wanted."

Did I? Did I really want to leave my friends, after we had been through so much and come so far? I'd been waiting for this day for ages, and now that it was actually here, I felt strange. Why wasn't I jumping for joy? Instead, I hesitated.

I looked at the faces of my new friends—Corky, Teresa, Robert, and the others. They wouldn't stand in my way, but they didn't really want me to leave, I could tell. To my surprise, I realized I didn't *want* to leave Room 24. Where else would I have true friends?

Now that I had learned to dance to new music, I didn't want to go back to the old routine. Next to Room 24, any other class would be horribly dull.

"Miss Hopkins!" I declared. "Cancel my transfer!"

"What?" She sounded incredulous. "You don't want to transfer? Why, I've heard nothing from you but your transfer since you came back to school. I thought you wanted to be in a regular class."

I wanted to tell her not to believe everything she heard, that my wanting to transfer was just a rumor.

"I'm in the *right* class," I said, grinning at my friends.

Together, laughing and punching one another good-naturedly, we walked up to the winners' platform to collect our trophy.

About the Author

CANDICE RANSOM is the author of over forty best-selling books for young readers, including picture books, biographies, and a four-book series for third graders. She has also written nearly one hundred articles and short stories for various magazines, including *Jack and Jill* and *Seventeen*. She lives in Centreville, Virginia, with her husband, Frank.